LIVING SANE
in a CRAZY WORLD

LOUJEANNE GUYE

ISBN 978-1-64468-921-9 (Paperback)
ISBN 978-1-64468-922-6 (Digital)

Covenant Books, Inc.
11661 Hwy 707
Murrells Inlet, SC 29576
www.covenantbooks.com

For my parents, Dennis and Leola Hamilton,
who modeled God's love for me.

To my family; my best friend Brenda Hamilton; and her
daughter Cassandra, my Loujeanne Guye Ministries team
members; my pastors, Bishop Thomas Dexter and Serita
Jakes; the other pastors who help mold me; and to all who ask
the question how can anyone live sane in a crazy world.

CHAPTER 1

"ISN'T MARRIAGE SUPPOSED to last a lifetime? If so, then why didn't mine?" Phyllis Whitmore muttered.

Tom Billings, Phyllis' lawyer, handed her the divorce decree. A grimace crossed her face as her slender hands clutched the papers that she just signed. Billings shoved copies of legal documents in his leather briefcase and snapped it shut on the heavy cherrywood courtroom table. "Good luck," he said politely.

"Thanks," Phyllis said with a lump in her throat and dabbed the corner of both eyes with her knuckles.

As Judge Clymer exited the chamber, her gaze lingered on Grayson as he hurried out of the courtroom. The chair scraped across the tile floor and she vaulted from it, scrambling to her feet after ending a seventeen-year marriage with Grayson Whitmore, CEO of Bruner and Bruner Engineering Corporation. Phyllis swerved around the table and dashed into the noisy hallway.

"Excuse me!" she said in a shaky voice to a man her shoulder had accidentally butted.

He gave her a half-lidded look, heaved a sigh, and darted into one of the courtrooms where other sobering and hopeless dismal dramas unfolded.

Phyllis made her descent down the spiral stairway in the rotunda. She briefly eyed the décor of the historic courthouse as she hurried to the lobby of the building. The entrance was grand with two broad white marble columns standing guard like soldiers at attention, but she thought the worn floor tiles, scarred wooden benches, and rickety elevators matched her mood more than the grand entrance. She hurried through the glass double doors of the courthouse downtown in Schenectady, New York, once known as the city that lights and hauls the world.

Both legs felt like they were strapped with lead as she descended each step. *Where is my light today?* Phyllis wondered. Even the weather was not on her side as the sky grew black. Jagged forks of lighting zigzagged across it while the rumble of thunderclaps could be heard in the distance before giant raindrops splattered against the asphalt. *Am I being punished?* she thought as she hiked to the uncovered parking lot. In a way, she was grateful for the summer shower that quickened her pace and disguised the tears that spilled down her oval-shaped face and honey brown complexion.

Earlier that morning, walking from the parking lot into the courthouse, she'd stared at a sky that was almost sapphire blue with its limitless depth. A hard lump formed in her throat that no amount of swallowing could remove. Either she buried her head in the sand or just missed all of the signs, she simply did not see the divorce coming. Now she must raise Randy and Chrissie alone. She heaved a deep breath while her thoughts trailed off to her kids. *Would Randy be able to cope? Thank God Chrissie has plenty of time to heal.*

Though she was impeccably dressed as always, clad in a navy blue suit trimmed with a gold button, she felt like yesterday's garbage that had been thrown in the trash…a total failure.

She punched the numbers of Randy's cell phone as her late model Lexus shot along Jay Street with the wipers swooshing across the windshield until the rain subsided. The black sky turned gray, hinting that the sun was about to peer through the sky again. Silver maple, elm, and pine trees waved gently in the warm breeze. Flowering petunias, hyacinths, lilacs and marigolds as golden as the sun's rays perfumed the air, proclaiming summer in full swing.

"Are you all right, Randy?" she asked.

"Uh, yeah, Mom. I'm all right," Randy replied in an unsteady voice. "But, Mom, Mr. Claremont's in our house. He wants to talk to you, like, now!"

Now? What has he done? Phyllis wondered, sighing heavily while waiting for Mr. Claremont to get on the line.

"Mrs. Whitmore, I'm afraid your son may be in a bit of trouble," he told her. "I can wait for you to get home, if you like."

"Thank you."

Phyllis pressed the gas pedal harder, and the car shot forward like a racehorse. Ten minutes later, she pulled into the tidy garage. She grabbed her purse, yanked the door open, and sprinted into the house. She brushed past a four-footed mosaic planter of ivy and a gigantic lily dangling in the air. George Claremont and her son were waiting in the living room.

"Tell me what's going on with Randy," Phyllis sighed and lowered herself on the circular leather sofa. She paid no attention to the grandfather clock chiming noon in the corner of the living room that had welcomed her into her glamorous home a thousand times before.

"Randy's a no-show twice. He hasn't kept up his appointment with me," Mr. Claremont drawled in his Southern dialect. "Besides that, he skipped school with two other boys in his class and were hanging out around the pool hall smoking cigarettes."

Phyllis leaped from the sofa. Hands shaky and arms flailing, she choked back more tears. "This is it, Randy! You're grounded *indefinitely!*" she barked.

"Aw, Mom! I was just *playin'* pool." Randy flipped several lengthy but neatly groomed braids over his broad shoulders. "For God's sake, I'm sixteen and a half!" A scowl creased his face as he bit his lower lip.

"Let's not get cocky, young man!" Phyllis exclaimed, looking up at Randy who was towering over her like a Georgia pine. As was her usual habit in her frustration, she clamped her hands on her hips.

"I'll let you handle your son, Mrs. Whitmore," Mr. Claremont said, rising to leave, "but call my secretary and schedule an appointment for Randy to meet with me soon."

Phyllis managed a nod, smile, and thanks as he left. Then she turned to stare Randy squarely in the eyes. "No more trouble. Okay, Randy?" she admonished.

"Sure, sure, Mom," Randy said, shrugging his shoulders, a tiny nose ring dangling on the end of his upturned nose. He then spun on

his heels, grabbed his MP3 player from the table, and placed an ear-
phone in each ear to drown out his mother's warnings before stomp-
ing to his room.

Phyllis quietly pushed the door open and softly stole into
Chrissie's room that night. A smile crossed her face and dimples
deepened in her cheeks as she saw her two-year-old daughter sleeping
peacefully. She gently kissed her toddler's forehead and pushed back a
few strands of Chrissie's curly locks, relieved that she did not have to
play or spend time with Chrissie before she could go to bed.

The divorce swooped down on her like a hawk descending
on an unsuspecting prey. As always, whenever life hit her like this,
Granny Mag's prayer echoed in Phyllis' mind. "Lord, let your hand
become my help," Granny Mag would pray.

Phyllis wondered if Grayson ever truly loved her. Grayson, the
charming, outspoken valedictorian of their college class, the one des-
tined for success and who promised he'd always be at her side. Her
mind wandered to less chaotic times during her college days when
she could have easily made another romantic choice, Brett Lancaster,
the shy all-star football player at Northern University who also promised to make her dreams come true.

The grandfather clock chimed midnight and brought Phyllis
back to reality. She raised her arms above her head and yawned. Her
eyes were heavy with sleep as her body ached all over. She clasped
both hands and whispered a prayer, leaving her cares in God's hands.
Then she crawled into bed, let her head sink into the pillow, and
closed her eyes.

"Life is a jumbled mess. How does anybody live a sane life in
this crazy world," she questioned before drifting off in a troubled
sleep.

CHAPTER 2

THE MEANDERING STREAMS of the Mohawk River snaked past the Stockade district where Phyllis' Dutch Colonial home was perched. Like the fast-flowing waters of the Mohawk, curving and turning with purpose, she wished she could handle the curves and turns of her life. Last night, her head swam like the river's foamy waters. Even her dream brimmed with activity.

> *Mom, like you, I'm stuck. A month after I was born and Daddy died, you were stuck raising me, George, Wylie, Kevin, and Oscar. The thing that I've always feared has come true. Mom, will Randy and Chrissie also have to go away and live with Granny, like I did, when you could no longer take care of us by yourself?*

"Mommy, Mommy!" Chrissie wailed in her toddler voice, waking her. She made a beeline through the doorway into Phyllis's bedroom, her usual Saturday morning routine. "Mommy, Mommy!" she whined again and raised one of Phyllis's eyelids to peer into her mother's half-lidded eye.

Phyllis yawned and glanced at the clock on the dresser, it read 6:00 a.m. Sunlight streamed through the window, splashing yellow light across the custom-made drapes. She quickly glanced at Grayson's empty space. *Alone. Some way to end a week and begin another*, she thought in a flash. She vowed to never love again.

"Hi, sweetie pie! How is my little angel?" She reached across the rumpled sheets and pulled Chrissie to her chest. A smile crossed Chrissie's face, showing a gap tooth. Phyllis hugged her and kissed her cheeks. A little hand tugged at Phyllis's arm.

"*I-side*, Mommy. *I-side*."

Champion jumped on the bed. A long wet tongue swept across Phyllis' face. She jerked away and chuckled as she wiped her damp cheek before patting the dog who was wagging his tail and yapping anxiously, also demanding to go outside.

"Mommy will take you *outside* when we go shopping. Let's eat first, okay?"

Phyllis slipped on a pink robe and donned a matching pair of slippers. She picked up Chrissie as she and Champion strode down the steps to the kitchen. Oversized mahogany cabinets circled the spacious kitchen. Antique bottles nestled between ivy. A mixture of other greenery cascaded over the top of the cabinets, accenting the red pots and pans dangling from the center island. Its granite top reminded Phyllis of tiny specks of sand as if she was enjoying life on the beach.

"Randy!" she yelled, pitching her voice to be heard from the kitchen to his bedroom upstairs. No answer came. She sighed and then hurried up the stairs into his bedroom, stumbling over clothes, CDs, and others items that screamed a teenager's room. "Randy!"

"Yeah, Mom?" he answered from under the sheet pulled over his face.

"Don't forget to make your appointment with Mr. Claremont's secretary this morning."

"I will, Mom. Oh, is Dad going?" Silence fell in the room. Randy added before Phyllis could answered him back. "He's working as *usual*, right?"

"Son, you know your father is no longer here with us."

"He didn't have to divorce me!" Randy yelled, a scowl creasing his face.

Feeling Randy's pain and frustration, her heart sank. Looking at him was like looking at Grayson. They had the same broad shoulders, handsome features, and warm brown eyes. She recalled Grayson's drive and determination that stemmed from his desire to not be like his father who was a drunk and an uncaring provider. Grayson became a workaholic. His whole life had been dominated by fear that he'd become a failure like his father.

"The office is open until noon. We need to meet with him today. All right, son?"

"C'mon, Mom, gimme a break. I'll call Claremont," he replied and pulled the sheet over his face.

"That's *Mr.* Claremont with a capital *M.* Call him. Hurry and get dressed. Breakfast will be ready shortly. After the visit with Mr. Claremont, I'm going shopping and around five o'clock I'm meeting some friends at Aperitivo Bistro."

"Fine," Randy said in an annoyed tone. He gathered the sheet in a ball and threw it at the foot of his bed. Then he quickly jumped out of bed and made his way to the shower.

Phyllis strode down the steps to the kitchen. She gave Chrissie a quick reassuring hug and plopped her in the high chair at the counter where she could keep an eye on her and Champion. She opened the fridge and grabbed a handful of breakfast foods in a hurry. The coffee pot gurgled and filled the room with the scent of Colombian coffee. Sometime later, she placed hot buttered biscuits, strips of bacon, scrambled eggs, and hash browns on the glass table. A cream-colored lily arrangement was set at the center of the table in a sparkling clear vase. Phyllis completed the breakfast spread with a small pitcher of orange juice and a jar of delectable marmalade on the table.

Her thoughts traveled to Grayson. *Is he having his usual cup of morning coffee about this time? Is he with another woman?*

The phone rang. Birdie Ratcliff, the caller ID flashed. The name made her want to make the sign of the cross on her chest. Birdie, as flighty as her name sounds, was nosy, sneaky, and undermining. Phyllis had avoided her calls for a couple of weeks. Now it was time to face the music.

"Hello?" Phyllis answered.

"Hi," the voice at the other end said. "What's going on, Phyllis? We haven't heard from you in a month. Are you still joining me, Charla, and Melissa for a girl's night out at Aperitivo Bistro this evening? They make the best Calamari, and I haven't had any in a while."

"Yes, I—"

"And by the way, how are you and Grayson?" Birdie was fishing for something. "How is *he* these days?" she asked in a coy voice.

"I definitely will not miss our girl's night out. I'll be there," Phyllis replied, keeping her cool.

"Look, Phyllis, I'm sorry about your divorce. Grayson—"

Phyllis sighed audibly. "Birdie, I'm in the middle of making breakfast. I'll see you tonight."

"You could have just said you were busy." Phyllis heard Birdie slammed the phone down.

How did she know about the divorce? Is this town so small that the news travels that fast? Did Grayson tell her? Would he spill the beans like that? If so, why? Something was wrong. What was really going on?

The smell of bacon wafted to Randy's room and enticed him to hurry downstairs. Chrissie eyed Randy and extended her hands out to him for him to take her out of her highchair. Randy stroked her chin and cracked a little smile before pulling himself to the table. Piling his plate high, he chomped on a piece of toast and chugged a glass of orange juice but toyed with most of his breakfast like a cat does with a mouse that he intends to eat later thinking about the inevitable meeting with his probation officer.

Phyllis enjoyed cooking and was thankful that it didn't pack any extra pounds on her 119-pound frame. After breakfast, she rinsed the dishes and loaded them into the dishwasher.

* * *

Phyllis pulled into Meredith's driveway and hit two short blasts on the horn to signal her arrival. She climbed out of the car with Chrissie and met Meredith at the door. A warm smile crossed Meredith's face bright as the flowering basket of petunias hanging in the front of her house. Meredith Hightower checked all the boxes in the friendship category. She and Phyllis had been close friends for a long time.

"Meredith, thanks a million for babysitting Chrissie."

"Anytime. You know how I love kids, especially Chrissie. She's a darling," said Meredith, tousling Chrissie's thick curly hair.

"Thanks. *You're* the darling!" Phyllis gave Meredith a warm embrace.

Meredith often kept Chrissie on weekends. She had been married a few years but had no children before her husband was killed by a drunk driver. She was only one year younger than Phyllis yet she seemed more mature and wiser. Could it be her relationship with God? Phyllis and God had been estranged for a long time, but she had plans to connect with Him again. Grayson never made time for church. It was a shame she allowed herself to stay away from God after her religious upbringing.

* * *

The car pulled on to State Street about twenty minutes later. Phyllis observed that Randy's shoulders were slumped and he kept his eyes lowered as they entered the probation office.

"How may I help you?" asked the secretary, peering from under her rimmed eyeglasses and glancing from Randy to Phyllis.

"My son, Randy Whitmore, has an appointment with Mr. Claremont."

"Mr. Claremont is with another client. He'll be with you shortly. Please be seated." She phoned him that his next appointment was waiting.

Ten minutes later, Mr. Claremont poked his head around the door of his office. "How are y'all this morning? Right this way," he said, shaking Phyllis' hand and patting Randy's shoulder, suggesting a hearty discussion was about to occur.

Randy entered Mr. Claremont's office with his head lowered as if it was pressed down by a heavy weight. Phyllis glanced at an inspirational plaque on the wall above Mr. Claremont's desk and hoped it suggested that he was understanding person.

"Please be seated," Mr. Claremont offered politely. He tilted his head and stared Randy in the eyes. "What can I do to help you to not miss your appointments?" Randy shrugged his shoulders and kept his gaze lowered, staring at the eccentric pattern of the carpet. "What are your goals, Randy? Your future depends on your education. Young man, tell me about your plans." Randy arched a brow and glanced up at Mr. Claremont but did not answer. "You're a bright young man but your truant behavior has you off the right path. Do you realize you've broken your probation and the negative effects that it has on your future or the burden it places on your family? I'm here to help you but you have to *allow* me to help you. Your whole life is ahead of you, however, the outcome is based on the decisions you make from now on...hopefully the right decisions. Well, what do you have to say for yourself?"

Randy wriggled around uneasily in his seat and eyed his probation officer a moment. Then he rubbed the bridge of his nose and snorted, "Nothin'."

"Randy, isn't there something that you'd like to tell Mr. Whitmore?" Phyllis urged.

"No, Mom." He lifted his shoulders in an I-don't-care-attitude, thinking, *Just get me out of here.*

"Mrs. Whitmore, I'm assigning Randy forty hours of community service. You may select an organization of your choice. Additionally, he must attend one hour of truancy training for a month."

Phyllis' heartbeat relaxed to a normal rhythm. "Is that clear, Randy?"

"Yeah, Mom," he said, ready to make an immediate beeline for the door.

"I'll see you in a week," said Mr. Claremont with a stern voice at Randy.

"Sir, yes, sir," Randy responded returning Mr. Claremont's gaze.

"Thanks," Phyllis said, thankful it was no worse for punishment as they left the probation office.

On their way home, Phyllis drove deep in thought. Relaxing on the passenger side of the car, Randy soon broke in on her thoughts.

"Mom, can I go to Proctors tonight? I promised Kerry we'd catch a movie this weekend." He waited for her response, hoping to determine the extent of his mother's anger.

"It's good to know that you and Kerry are no longer butting heads."

"We're cool."

"All right, if you promise to stay out of trouble. Be home by ten o'clock."

"Ten thirty," Randy negotiated. "Mom, I'll need some cash too."

With a single hand, Phyllis managed to open her purse and pull out several bills that she handed to him. Then she held out her lanky arms widely to quickly hug him.

"C'mon, Mom! I'm not a baby," he said with a sheepish grin.

Phyllis' dimples deepened, gleaming a half-smile.

Randy pulled up the keypad on his cell phone and texted Kerry Mitterson, the girl he'd been glued to for months. "I'm on my way," the message affirmed.

* * *

"Let's go," Randy exclaimed as Kerry ran to meet him.

Her jeans looked like they had been painted on her wiry frame. She sashayed to the end of the sidewalk and wrapped her arms around Randy's neck, flashing her large brown eyes. A wisp of an ebony curl dangled from her round face. Kerry fingered several of Randy's lengthy braids, pursed her lips, and planted a hot kiss on his lips.

"Come on!" yelled Kyle Sumrall from the driver's seat of his car. Lela Everette was stuffed beside him, giggling and puffing a cigarette.

Randy pulled one from his back pocket and lit it. He blew puffs of smoke into Kerry's face who was also giggling like a hyena. The car sped along the tree-lined streets, tires squealing. They drove past Proctors Theater like a bombshell and headed to the club on the other side of town.

* * *

Phyllis quickly completed her shopping, which was easier without Chrissie. She glanced at her watch. It read 4:45 p.m. It was time to head for Apertivio Bistro. She entered the restaurant through the double doors. Ocean blue light danced and shimmered from candles hung in equal distance on a long brick wall, accentuating the soft padded blue chairs. Phyllis spotted Charla Myerson and made a beeline to the table where she was sitting with Melissa Guvenstaf and Birdie, sipping their soft drinks and yakking like cackling hens.

"May I take your order please?" a friendly waitress asked as they eyed the menu.

Birdie made a hungry growl before ordering. "I'll have the calamari, stuffed portobello mushrooms, and a spinach salad."

"The prosciutto-wrapped salmon and a Caesar salad will be fine for me," said Phyllis.

"I'd like the mini rigatoni Bolognese," requested Charla, "and another glass of tea."

"Coming right up," acknowledged the waitress and scooted through the door to place their orders. A short while later, she brought the piping hot orders to the wooden table.

After idle chatter and a discussion of the latest fashion news, Birdie changed the conversation. "Phyllis, how are you these days?" she asked, smirking.

Phyllis smiled and shrugged. "Oh, you know, same old song, different verse."

The waitress eyed the near empty cups and filled them with a second round of coffee. Phyllis fiddled with her napkin and took a sip of coffee.

"So how does it feel to be a free woman, Phyllis? Your divorce—"

"Divorced?" Charla and Melissa chimed in unison. "We're sorry, Phyllis. We didn't know."

Phyllis shifted her gaze from Charla and Melissa and narrowed her eyes at Birdie. She steadied her voice. "I think I feel sick to my stomach but the food is great. It must be your company, Birdie!" With that, she stormed out of the restaurant.

CHAPTER 3

PHYLLIS HAD A lot on her mind when she left Aperitivo Bistro, angry at Birdie. She parked her car in the garage and momentarily slammed the door on her memory of the scene at the restaurant. Keys jingled in the lock as she let herself into the posh family room through the garage. Champion barked from inside the house and met her at the door.

"Hello, Champion," said Phyllis, a gentle smile tugging at the corner of her mouth.

He bounded around her legs and wagged his tail briskly from side to side. She hunkered down on her knees on the ceramic tile. Champion leaped in her arms, sweeping a wet tongue several times up and down her face. She cuddled him while running her palm over his head and down his silky ears. He stared at her steadily for a couple of minutes, and his gaze bore into her conscience.

"You're a real champion." The dog looked at her as if he understood. Phyllis welcomed his affection. In some ways, it reminded her of family and the unconditional love and companionship of someone waiting for her when she walked through the door at night. It wasn't "Honey, I'm home," but a wagging tail that lifted her spirit. That would be much better than the silence that now greeted her. *Dogs are not like humans*, she thought. *They love unconditionally!* She placed him in the doggie bed and tossed him a rubber bone. He gave her a forlorn look and nosed the bone and played with it.

Phyllis eyed her watch. Randy wouldn't be home for several hours. Her thoughts flashed again to Birdie. She quickly dismissed the thought from her mind as her stomach gurgled and growled, reminding her of the uneaten meal at the restaurant. Putting her purse on the granite counter, she walked to the refrigerator and selected a container of deli ham and condiments. Shaved ham was piled between two slices of bread, lettuce, cheese, pickle and a smidgen of light mayonnaise. She plopped ice cubes into a glass of cola that fizzed and brimmed over the top.

Glancing around, Phyllis spotted a certified letter and a stack of unopened mail sandwiched between two canisters at the end of the counter. A frown wrinkled her forehead as she ripped open the certified letter addressed from Fidelity of Schenectady. The bold words glared at her like sparkles on the Fourth of July. "Third Notice: Payment must be received immediately to avoid foreclosure." Shock rippled through her veins. The half-eaten sandwich plummeted to the floor.

"Is this a mistake?" she asked herself. "Hadn't Grayson paid the mortgage and the other bills?"

"I'll take care of our finances and pay the bills," he said early in their marriage.

It was an agreement that worked all right…until now. A wrinkle crossed her forehead as Phyllis trudged across the kitchen and down the hall to the den. Soft light fell across the room through the yellow damask curtains glinting golden rays on a framed puzzle of Lawrence, the Indian statue, respected and beloved by Schnectadians. It hung above an oversized reddish-brown leather recliner that seemed to beckon her to put her feet up and relax. If only her life could fit together like the framed pieces of the puzzle that hung above the recliner. Would she ever know what it meant to relax again? She flung herself facedown on a love seat angled on a wall across from the recliner. Her chest rose and fell with uncontrollable sobs. A few minutes later, her cell phone chimed to the tune of America the Beautiful. She let the phone ring several times before answering.

"Hello?" she answered in a whisper, trying to disguise her sobs.

"Phyllis, my dear, this is Mrs. Creighton. I'm calling to remind you about our upcoming meeting for the annual Stockade Walkabout and Waterfront Faire," said an elderly voice. "Folks will be pouring in from around the world to see our historic homes and tour our scenic gardens again. I'm heading the committee. We'd appreciate your help this year."

"Of...of course." Phyllis tried to carefully respond in a controlled tone.

"Thanks, dearie. I'll call you again soon."

Phyllis consented to help with the preparations only to quickly end the conversation with Mrs. Creighton. She could feel herself going into her shell...clamming up, unwilling to deal with *anything* or *anyone*, and shutting down as she often did when the road got rough. Tears bubbled up in her eyes and rolled down her face. When she dialed the number of the bank to check on the account balance, it said insufficient funds! First, the stupid divorce and unpaid bills, now she had a delinquent mortgage. It was too much! She'd grown up believing that marriage was a promise to God, but then God promised to love her and care for her but He hadn't seemed to be holding up His part of the bargain. Certainly not with her marriage anyway.

* * *

Meredith's doorbell chimed. She peered through the window by the doorway and smiled as she spotted Phyllis at the door.

"Hi," Phyllis greeted, entering the house with renewed composure. The aroma of chocolate, cinnamon, and other spices wafted in the air.

"Chrissie's asleep in the guest room," Meredith said, beaming a Mona Lisa smile while enveloping Phyllis with a quick embrace. Chocolate chip cookies hot out of the oven." Meredith said, leading the way toward the kitchen.

"No thanks." Phyllis slowly walked beside Meredith past two Dutch chairs reclined toward the other. When she entered the kitchen, Phyllis plopped down on the padded kiwi-colored chair. A crystal centerpiece and a few other accessories graced the dining table with its mahogany wood finish.

"You never refuse your favorite cookies, Phyll, even when my oven ruins them." She poked fun, but Phyllis seemed to miss the joke. "Is something bothering you?" Meredith asked, staring at Phyllis through soft brown eyes fingering her cropped, ebony hair. "You seemed tense, concerned."

Meredith's question struck Phyllis between the eyes. She tried to hide her feelings but she guessed she hadn't done a very good job. "It's just life. Nothing you can do anything about."

"True, but we have help. God wants to help you," said Meredith, rising from her chair to comfort Phyllis with a sisterly embrace.

Meredith and Phyllis had been close friends since high school. Phyllis could trust and always confide in her. She told Meredith about Grayson and her divorce; the incident at the restaurant with Birdie; the unpaid bills; and, more importantly, the delinquent mortgage payment as well as the requirement to find an organization for Randy to complete his hours of community work.

Phyllis cupped her face in her hands as hot tears streamed down her face. "How does one stay sane in this crazy mixed-up world?" she whimpered.

"The Lord promised to keep our hearts in perfect peace if we keep our minds focused on Him," answered Meredith. She clasped Phyllis' hands and offered to pray. Phyllis nodded in agreement and closed her eyes as Meredith began to pray. "Lord, we don't understand your purpose. We don't even know why we always face trials, but we're assured that You are with us through it all. Father, we thank You for every blessing and for our friendship and love this day. We ask you to please place your loving hand on our lives and guide us. Amen."

"Amen," fell from Phyllis' lips while the prayer washed over her. Smoothing the ruts from her and her kids' lives was her goal. "Thanks," Phyllis said, extending her arms around Meredith.

"My mom once told me the legend of the Cherokee Indian youth's rite of passage. Sometimes when I'm faced with difficult situations, I remember the story. It points me back to the promises of God. Would you like to hear the story?"

"Sure," Phyllis responded in an appreciative tone.

"A father takes his young son into the forest, blindfolds him, and leaves him alone. The son is required to sit on a stump the whole night and not remove the blindfold until the morning sun shines through it. He cannot cry out for help to anyone. Once he survives the night, he is a man. He cannot tell the other boys of this experience because each boy must come into manhood on his own. The boy is naturally terrified. He can hear all kinds of noises from wild beasts all around him. The wind blows the grass and earth and shakes his stump, but he sits stoically, never removing the blindfold. It is the only way he can become a man! Finally, after a horrific night, the sun appears. When he removes his blindfold, he discovers his father sitting on the stump next to him. He had been watching the entire night, protecting his son from harm. We, too, are never alone. Even when we don't know it, God is watching over us, sitting on the stump beside us. When trouble comes, all we have to do is reach out to Him." Meredith assured Phyllis, "God's loving arms are outreached to you."

Phyllis beamed a smile as the idea warmed her. That's what she needed, loving arms to hold her close and guard her against hurt and evil.

CHAPTER 4

A SMILE CROSSED Phyllis' face and a faint grin lingered on her lips while she reminisced about Meredith and her conversation earlier that evening. Meredith's words were like medicine, healing and soothing her. She felt like a ball and chain had been removed from her legs for a brief moment.

Chrissie let out a sleepy yawn, toddling beside Phyllis as they entered the house. Phyllis gave Chrissie a snack and dressed her for bed.

"Good night, Precious," she said as she kissed Chrissie on both cheeks and wrapped her arms around her for a warm hug.

"Nighty-night, Mommy." Chrissie puckered her lips and gave Phyllis a smack on the face.

Phyllis thought about Randy but did not expect him soon since he promised to return around ten thirty. A few hours later, Phyllis fell asleep on the sofa downstairs while reading a Grace Livingston Hill novel. The automatic light switch on the lamp turned itself off. The grandfather clock cornered in the living room chimed its tune for midnight, but Phyllis did not hear it in her dream world.

Randy flipped a dangling braid away from his face at exactly 12:30 a.m. and used his key to unlock the front door. He stole softly into the house and ignored the light switch that allowed his eyes to adjust to the dusky light in the den. He glanced around the room but did not see his Mom still asleep on the sofa. Then he tried to tiptoe to his room with care where soiled clothes, DVDs, CDs, and other gadgets lay sprawled across the hardwood floor. In his clumsy attempt to remain quiet, a vase tumbled down and made a loud thud in the silence.

"Was that Champion looking for Chrissie?" Phyllis assumed, half raising her body on the sofa. She grabbed her cell that she put down beside her and peered at the time, 12:30 a.m. "Randy!" Phyllis hollered in a shrill voice. No answer. Hearing a clamor from his bedroom, she called him again, her voice booming up the stairs, "Randy!" Still no answer. A frown crinkled her face and Phyllis trudged up the stairs to his room. "You're late! Where have you been, young man?"

"Yeah, Mom. Sorry, I—I'm a *little* late," he said apologetically.

"I can handle my math better than that, and I know you can too. It's 12:30 a.m., not, 10:30 p.m., the time you promised you'd be back. America is still beautiful. Don't let this happen again, Randy Alexander Whitmore!" Phyllis said, clamping her hands on her hips.

"Yeah, Mom," he replied with a chuckle, one that Phyllis didn't hear. Randy understood that *America is still beautiful* meant that he should have called Phyllis on her cell phone, which rang to the tune of "America the Beautiful."

"We'll deal with this some more tomorrow," Phyllis said and headed down the stairs to dress for bed. A foul smell wafted under her nose. *What is that scent?* She sniffed. *Is that smoke? Beer?* Anger and frustration raged inside her—anger at Grayson, frustration with Randy.

Randy was growing wild. While lying in bed, she could not get away from the memory of the smell of smoke and beer in his room. She shuddered involuntarily as she thought of this. Randy, her oldest child and only son, scarcely grown out of childhood. Randy, of whom she had always been so proud, gone wrong so early. He had not been raised like this. Phyllis released a puff of air from between her lips as she settled herself in bed and tried to sleep in the midst of the turmoil of her mind.

* * *

Monday morning was as hectic as ever. Phyllis wrapped a black-and-gold scarf around her neck and draped it over her black suit. She reached down and picked Chrissie up in her arms while rushing into the kitchen.

"That *wun*," Chrissie pointed to the Lucky Charms cereal when Phyllis reached for the Kix.

Although it didn't seem possible, Phyllis hoped her life would be like a lucky charm today. She poured the cereal in a small bowl and splashed milk over it.

Randy ran down the stairs with a pencil behind his ear and paper in hand. He popped two slices of bread into the toaster and poured himself a large glass of orange juice. "Morning, Mom," he said quickly, hoping Phyllis had forgotten about last night.

"Good morning. Call me when you get to school," she mandated in a sharp tone.

Randy gulped his juice in a hurry. "Call?" he said. "Gosh, Mom! I'm not five years old."

"Five or fifty, you'd better call," warned Phyllis. Randy bolted out of the house like a rodeo steer let out of a stall to catch the school bus to Schenectady High. Although Phyllis had never been a woman who stormed and raged, that seemed to change overnight like her circumstances. She must be firm with Randy, she thought.

A half hour later, Phyllis turned onto Washington Street at Lil Tots Daycare. Flowering trees lined the street and perfumed the air with sweet fragrances with pink, lavender, and yellow buds. She parked the car in one of the assigned parking spaces in front of the red brick building. Huge brightly colored alphabets artfully adorned the chain-link fence around the playground.

Chrissie's eyes widened when she saw and heard other toddlers flowing into the daycare with their parents. "I get out, Mommy?" she said in an eager childish voice.

A smile crossed Phyllis' face as she slid off the seat of the Lexus and opened the door. She released the child lock, opened the rear passenger door, and carefully lifted Chrissie out of the car. With Chrissie at her side, holding her hand, they strolled into the daycare.

"Hello, Mrs. Whitmore," said Mrs. O'Neil in a cordial voice.

"Good morning!" Phyllis returned the greeting with a dimpled smile.

Mrs. O'Neil, Chrissie's teacher, glanced at Chrissie and bent down to hug her. "Hi, Precious—"

Chrissie ignored Mrs. O'Neil's affection when she eyed another toddler playing with her favorite toy. She tore away from Mrs. O'Neil's embrace and sped across the room like a sprinter at the sound of the gun. "Mine!" cried Chrissie, yanking the doll from the other toddler's hands.

"That's not nice," cautioned Mrs. O'Neil who handled the outburst with the attention and discipline of a professional.

Chrissie whimpered. Phyllis kissed and consoled her and then signed the daily attendance log to check Chrissie into the day care. Phyllis left and whisked to the car to take the shortest route to work.

CHAPTER 5

THE OFFICE OF Monterey and Cleary came into view. Phyllis opened the beveled glass door of the lobby and ambled across the marble floor past the circular receptionist desk.

"Good morning," Phyllis said with a bright smile and friendly voice. Trekking the usual path to her office, she greeted Elena, the receptionist seated behind a large antique cherrywood desk with artful designs lining the walls.

"Hello, Mrs. Whitmore," Elena said, her rouged smeared lips curved into a welcoming smile on her freckled face. "Have a nice day!" She greeted Phyllis with mirth.

"Thanks, Elena," Phyllis said back with mutual warmth. She turned a corner and steered her steps toward the elevator.

Jerome the security guard stood a few feet away, manning his post near the elevator. He beamed a broad smile as Phyllis approached him, which was his usual manner. "How are you on this fine day?" he asked, bowing like a gentleman and an officer from his days of service in the marines.

"Fine, thank you," Phyllis replied in a friendly tone.

For the past seven years, both of them were magnificent employees who portrayed the high standards of the Monterey and Cleary Company. Phyllis appreciated their friendly countenance, which brightened her early morning arrival and added warmth to the atmosphere of the work environment.

She entered the glass elevator and punched the numbers for the seventeenth floor. A sweeping panoramic view of Schenectady could be seen from certain angles as she peered out the glassy tube skyrocketing upward. Like the elevator, she wished her life was heading up and not down. Phyllis eyed her watch, nine o'clock. There was still no call from Randy! A frown furrowed on her brow as she bit her lower lip. She'd call on her break, an hour and a half away. Her decision calmed her edgy emotions. A lot of things lingered on her mind, including tying up some loose ends concerning Randy's community service. In fact, it was tops on her list of things to do.

After the elevator came to a stop on the seventeenth floor, Phyllis stepped out of it and ambled along the lavish hallway. A heady smell of Jasmine perfume lingered in the air and hit her in the face. It made her want to hold her breath. Eloisa must have already gotten to work ahead of her. She was known for dousing the office of her fragrance. She continued down the hallway and tuned her ears to the soothing rhythmic notes of the background music. In a few steps, Phyllis entered the brightly lit spacious office that contained a comfortable mixture of modern and traditional furniture. She plopped her purse in the desk drawer. After a short while, she settled down at the desk and then got up and sauntered to the break room to make a cup of coffee.

"Good morning," Karen and Eloisa echoed in unison, greeting Phyllis as they passed her on the way to their workstations. Eloisa's perfume irritated her nostrils. She wanted to wrinkle her nose but held back until she moved past them. The office teemed with other co-workers bristling like soldier ants on a mission.

"Hello," Phyllis replied with a dimpled smile and a half chuckle. She watched Karen and Eloisa shifting their gaze from one to the other, engaging in chatter and letting out soft bursts of laughter.

Phyllis returned to her desk with a steaming cup of coffee and sank in her seat. She eyed her watch dial gleamed 9:35 a.m. Searching frantically for Randy's cell number, she dug into her designer purse for her phone, tapped the screen lightly with her index finger, and rang Randy's phone. He didn't answer her several calls. Frustrated, she hung up. She'd try to reach him and an organization regarding the community service later. Phyllis swiveled around and lowered her chair to reach the bottom drawer of the file cabinet in the desk. She opened it and withdrew a folder labeled "Annual Financial Projections." As she raised herself up and spun around in the chair, she caught a glimpse of the framed family portrait. The snapshot of Grayson (handsome and debonair as ever), Randy, Chrissie, and herself in a happier moment was the centerpiece on the modular desk. *A reflection of love and unity*, she thought. She'd soon remove the framed photograph and replace it with only Randy and Chrissie. For now, she'd leave it on her desk. Phyllis cupped both hands on her face, musing over the reality of her first day of work as a single mom. She'd reveal the news later.

"Rally the troops, Lil," Rylander, her boss, said, scampering to his office like a squirrel racing to hide acorns for the winter, "meeting at ten."

"Will do," answered Lil Moreno, hurrying to pass the word to ensure everyone's attendance.

A few minutes later, the enticing smell of coffee wafted throughout the office.

Phyllis pressed the on button of the computer. Shortly after, the monitor screen displayed the desktop of multiple icons. She clicked the e-mail icon and read several of them before she saw the one from Rylander that was marked urgent, "Staff meeting ten o'clock at conference room F-1 west. Please be prompt."

Phyllis made a mental note of the meeting as she sipped her coffee and shuffled through a wad of papers from the folder.

"Good morning, Phyllis," Birdie said in a singsong tone. She stood in front of Phyllis's desk, seemingly appearing out of nowhere. Birdie smirked at Phyllis as if she found an unsuspected prey. She apparently came from the secretary's cubicle where she dropped off a sealed envelope designated for the chief financial officer. She realized that Phyllis wouldn't be able to see her from that vantage point.

Phyllis drew in a long breath. "What little birdie flew you here? Who in the name of common sense unlocked your cage?" Phyllis asked, sarcastically glancing up at Birdie without blinking an eye. Birdie irked her to the core.

"Let's just say—"

Phyllis jumped from her chair and faced Birdie, trying not to arouse attention and to remain professional. "Isn't it time you fly south, Birdie?" she said pointedly, interrupting Birdie's conversation. Phyllis's patience had reached its limits. "We both know what you're up to with your diabolical scheming. It won't work. Divorce is no new secret, and *my divorce* is my personal business. People wouldn't be interested in *your* version of the story anyway. Get lost."

Birdie gasped! Her eyes widened and her hands flew to her mouth. She spun on her heels and stormed out of the room like a bolt of lightning zigzagging across an angry sky.

"Ouch!" Lil yelped as Birdie tore past her, brushing her shoulder with unintentional but direct force. She straightened herself and whirled around to watch Birdie dash out of the office without offering an apology.

Hearing the commotion, Phyllis turned her head in that direction and observed that Lil had her eyes on her from where she sat. Lil made a mad dash to Phyllis' desk like a child seeking parental attention after receiving a cut or scrape from a fall. "Who ruffled her tail feathers?" Lil asked Phyllis, gently massaging her shoulder.

"Just being herself," answered Phyllis. "Another example of Birdie's cocky attitude and self-importance on display," she said matter-of-factly.

"I see," Lil said. She shook her head from side to side in disbelief and quickly dismissed the incident. "Oh, by the way, staff meeting at ten o'clock. Usual place."

"What's the meeting about?" A curious look crossed Phyllis' face.

"Not sure, but I believe it's about the Fontnel project that Rylander briefly discussed last week during our midweek staff meeting or maybe something about the global petroleum enterprise contract. We're about to find out," she said with a shrug of her shoulder.

"Okay. Thanks, Lil." A few minutes before ten, Phyllis darted from her desk and joined the other staff as they sauntered to the posh conference room.

In a let's-get-down-to-business manner, Rylander promptly began the meeting. "You may recall that during our staff meeting last week, I emphasized that there is a lot of ground to be covered before the Fontnel project contract can be signed," he said, seated at the head of the triangular cherrywood table while his five-member team sat comfortably on leather swivel chairs. "Keep in mind that this is a multi-million-dollar contract that other asset management companies have also placed their bids on. We need to be on our p's and q's and on point throughout the entire process. Is that clear?"

"Yes," they replied, glancing at each other.

Rylander preferred to be called by his surname and called others by theirs. He possessed the business acumen of any well-known financial giant. In the financial world, William Barrett Rylander, at the age of forty-four, was no lightweight. He was undoubtedly successful and focused on staying at the top. Keeping true to his habit, he stroked his chin contemplatively and fanned his fingers through a thick mane of curly ebony hair. "We'll need to form teams," he said.

Phyllis doodled on her writing pad as her mind drifted while she perched at the luxurious conference table. Although she gave Rylander a steady glance, her mind was a thousand miles away. Today she did not notice the lean chiseled features of his face, his trim muscular build, or the bronze complexion that complimented his overall look.

Rylander leaned back in his chair, folded his arms across his chest, and began delegating individual tasks to complete the project. "Van Nieman, review Fontnel's financial portfolio from cover to cover."

"Sure," Van Nieman responded. His body language seemed to shout, "I can handle it!"

"Wilson, you and Roberson check the company's financial habits for the last five years. Have they been conservative or aggressive spenders? Give the company the once-over. You know, our usual procedure." Wilson nodded in agreement. Roberson flipped a thumbs-up, acknowledging his consent. "Lil, prepare an executive portfolio for each of the Fontnel's top executives."

"Will do," she countered, engaging him with her favorite expression.

"Phyllis, schedule a meeting with counsel and handle the legal work." She did not immediately respond as her thoughts were elsewhere. For a brief moment, Rylander shot her a questioning look. His deep voice brought her back to reality and she noticed the puzzled look on his face.

"Oh, of course," Phyllis acknowledged belatedly, trying to recover her composure.

Rylander rose, unfolding his lanky stature and faced them. "That's all for now. We'll follow up next week. Be prepared to give your progress reports." he said, dismissing the hour-long meeting.

Separately, they scattered to their cubicles. Phyllis headed for the break room to call Randy. She tapped his number on the screen and listened impatiently. The dial tone sounded after more than three rings and no answer. *He better has a good reason*, she thought and went back to her desk.

* * *

Randy shuffled through his school corridor to his locker. He opened it; chucked his math, history, and English textbooks inside for his scheduled morning classes; and slammed the locker door shut. Long braids swayed around his shoulders as he sped down the hallway. His oversized white polo shirt and denim jeans blended in with what the other Schenectady High School kids sported.

Students were swarming the hallway, flowing into and out of the classrooms and chattering about everything under the sun. Corey Littleton spotted Randy from the back and scrambled to catch up with him.

"What's up?" Corey asked, pulling alongside Randy who towered over much of the crowd. He flashed a set of white teeth.

Randy grinned. Without hesitation, he gave Corey a fist-bump. They plodded up the noisy hallway. Above the loud noise and commotion, Randy heard his cell phone ring.

"Aren't you going to answer the phone?" Corey asked, halting for a moment with a quizzical look on his face.

"Nah, it's probably my mom," Randy answered nonchalantly. "She'll be furious, but she'll get over it."

"My mom would kill me if I pulled a stunt like that."

"It's all right!" Randy snapped. A scowl settled over his face as he clambered up the steps to the classroom on the second floor, leaving Corey bewildered.

CHAPTER 6

LIL MORENO STROLLED down the aisle to Phyllis' desk. "Thanks for helping me line up the information for the executive portfolio. It was thoughtful of you," she said, a glow on her face.

"You're welcome, Lil."

Phyllis glanced up at the clock on the wall and occasionally watched the time. When its fingers pointed at five o'clock sharp, she wasted no time finishing her work. She quickly powered off the computer, grabbed her purse, and rushed out of the office. The elevator door slammed her in the face in her haste. When it stopped at the seventh floor, it was crammed with people flocking home. She managed to squeeze in and press the button for the ground floor where her car was parked in the covered garage. The moment she got off the elevator, stuffy air blasted her in the face with a hint of gas fumes. Phyllis winced and quickened her pace to her car. As she slid into the driver seat, a cool breeze stirred loose strands of her hair over her shoulders when she turned on the air conditioner full blast. Flipping the sun visor down, she put on her rimmed sunglasses and headed west onto State Street.

The car sped along like a race car as Phyllis hurried to pick Chrissie up from the day care. Maples and pines dotted the periphery, swaying to the gentle summer breeze. The late afternoon sun shimmered off the hood of her car like sparkling diamonds. Since that morning, the temperature had risen considerably. So had her anxiety. Phyllis' mind whirred with the events of the day. Her to-do-list was longer than she cared to think about or deal with for that matter. Then her thoughts flashed to Randy. She'd set some things straight with him tonight, she thought, and tried to mentally brace herself for his negative reaction.

On a positive note, a smile tugged at the corner of her mouth as she reflected on the tirade with Birdie the other day. She stood up to her and hoped that she put her in her place for good. She was proud of herself. Birdie had always been annoying. Most of the time, people avoided her like a rattlesnake in strike position.

Close to the day care, a driver blasted his horn as her car wandered into the other lane for a brief moment, distracted by her thoughts. It jolted her back to reality. Gripping the steering wheel, she maneuvered the sleek car into the proper lane again. Beads of perspiration dampened Phyllis' hands as she walked from the car into Lil Tots Daycare. Children's artwork hung on either side of the walls. Red, yellow, orange, purple, and other hues filled the room with bright colors. Toys were nestled in one corner and a reading center stationed along the back wall displayed books stacked on low shelves.

Mrs. Glover, the office assistant, glanced up from her keyboard as Phyllis entered the room. "Good afternoon, Mrs. Whitmore." Mrs. Glover lips curved into an amiable smile. Phyllis returned a warm smile then dug into her purse to retrieve her driver's license, a school policy to ensure the safety of their children. "Please sign the log," Mrs. Glover requested in a congenial tone.

After Phyllis scribbled her name on the sheet, she saw Chrissie drawing squiggles on a sheet of construction paper. As soon as Chrissie saw Phyllis, she picked up her paper and tore across the room, colliding into her with full force.

"Hi, Mommy!" she yelled, clinging to Phyllis and holding up the paper for her to see.

"Hello, darling." Phyllis picked her up and gave her a bear-hug.

"It's a *budderfly*, Mommy." Chrissie's eyes brightened.

"What a beautiful budderfly!" Phyllis mimicked. Her lips skewed into a grin while taking Chrissie's hand. "It's beautiful just like you!"

As usual, Champion could be heard barking inside the house whenever he heard the key turning in the lock. After Phyllis parked the car in the garage, she and Chrissie entered the house. Champion met them at the door, yapping and wagging his tail. A smile etched her face as she watched Champion who was ready to play. Chrissie and the dog both scuttled to a corner. Champion crouched on the tile floor on all four, nuzzling Chrissie as she cuddled with him. Chrissie stroked Champion, running her palms over its head and down its short shaggy ears. He whimpered and drew a long wet tongue across her face. She and Champion entertained themselves in their own playful worlds.

Phyllis plucked the cell phone from her purse and said to Christie, "Mommy's going upstairs. Stay and play with Champion till I come back." She headed upstairs to her room and changed into comfortable clothes. A few minutes later, she came downstairs and discovered Chrissie and Champion running around the room.

Randy barged into the family room a short time later, his ear glued to the cell phone and motioning with his hands as he talked. He ambled straightway to the refrigerator and poured orange juice in a tumbler. When he saw his mom, he muttered a quick hello and started to scamper to his room.

"Whoa!" Phyllis called out. "You've got some explaining to do, young man. You didn't call me this morning or answered my phone calls?" Still holding the tumbler in his hand, Randy stood in front of his mom in stark silence but staring her directly in the eyes. "Don't give me that dear-in-the-headlights look," she cautioned in a frustrated tone.

The silence lingered briefly. "Sorry, Mom. I didn't hear my phone," he shrugged.

"I asked for an explanation, not an excuse, Randy, Don't let this happen again," she said in a huff on her way to the kitchen.

"Okay, Mom." Randy gulped the rest of the juice, tossed the tumbler in the sink, and stomped upstairs to his room. A loud *thump* echoed as he closed his door.

"Snack, Mommy?" Chrissie asked, wrapping around Phyllis' legs.

Phyllis grabbed an orange from the fruit bowl and peeled a few slices for Chrissie, which she readily shared with Champion. She did not want to cook dinner today. Part of her wanted to put her feet up and relax. She decided on making a sandwich. She pulled out packages of chopped ham, chicken breast, and lettuce from the refrigerator. Smearing mayonnaise on slices of wheat bread, the sandwiches were topped off with condiments, pickle slices, and potato chips. Then Phyllis added ice cubes into a pitcher of lemonade.

Loud music boomed throughout the house. It didn't take much to annoy her today. Ticked off, she dashed to Randy's room.

"What's up, Mom?" her son asked.

Phyllis struggled not to clamp both of her hands on her hips. "Could you turn the volume down on the TV?"

Randy grabbed the TV remote control beside him where he lay sprawled on the bed to lower the volume, wondering what the big deal was.

After dinner, Phyllis read stories from some of Chrissie's favorite books then dressed her and tucked her in bed. She drew in a lengthy breath as she plopped down on a chair in the family room feeling dejected, Phyllis' cupped her face with both hands. Randy was in his own teenage world and Chrissie was sound asleep.

She thought about preparing a budget, which was top on her list also, but first she had to find and contact an organization where Randy could perform his community service. She could feel herself retreating into her shell, not having to deal with *anything* or *anyone*. This became a typical characteristic of Phyllis when her anxiety level reached a boiling point. Loneliness seemed to engulf her as tears ran down her oval-shaped face. *Change, just accept it,* she thought. *The only thing permanent in life is death.*

* * *

After Bible study, Meredith went straight home. No sooner than she entered the house, the phone rang.

"Hello?" Meredith answered the caller.

"This is Mrs. Creighton. Will you be able to work on the committee for our annual Walkabout Faire this year?"

"I'll be glad to," Meredith assured her. "Count me in."

"I have not been able to reach Phyllis Whitmore. She's not answering her home or cell phone. Let me know if you contact her please. Thanks, Meredith."

"Sure," replied Meredith before she hung up the phone. Concern grew on her face. Meredith dialed Phyllis' cell number. No answer. *So unlike Phyllis to not answer*, Meredith thought. She wondered if Phyllis was okay, remembering how distraught she was about her circumstances. She dialed the number again. Still no answer. A frown crossed her face. Meredith flexed her wrist and checked the time, only seven o'clock.

She backed the car out of the garage and headed to Phyllis' house to make sure everything was all right. The timing was perfect anyway since she planned on visiting her to drop off some things she bought for Chrissie, an ivory satin dress adorned with five miniature roses set in the waist dotted with pearls around the neckline. The dress still hung in the plastic wrap from the department store. It seemed to be tailor-made for Chrissie. A second bag was filled with toys fit for a toddler's pleasure. Putting the thought of the dress aside, she needed to be assured that Phyllis was all right. Stopping by her house tonight would kill two birds with one stone. Meredith pulled into Phyllis' driveway at around seven thirty.

Phyllis lit up like the Fourth of July when she saw Meredith. She needed a diversion from the stress in her life. She hugged Meredith and invited her to come in and join her at the kitchen table for coffee. Meredith carried the two bags on her arm.

"Mrs. Creighton and I have been trying to reach you concerning the annual Walkabout and Waterfront Faire next month. She needs our help. Anyway, I thought I'd come over and check on you and the kids." Meredith handed the bags to Phyllis.

"Thanks, you've made my day!" Phyllis said, giving her another gracious hug. "Chrissie will love her dress and toys." She put them on the back of the sofa as they strode to the kitchen.

The last time Mrs. Creighton called, Phyllis agreed to help with the preparations only to get her quickly off the phone. Her mood was no better tonight. "Excuse me, Meredith," said Phyllis and leaped from her chair to get her cell phone that she forgot she'd silenced earlier.

Meredith sensed that something was wrong. Phyllis was cordial but seemed to be preoccupied. She watched her leave the room. *Her phone was silenced. Who or what was it she didn't want to talk about?* An unsettling feeling washed over her. Before her thoughts cleared, Phyllis entered the kitchen with her cell phone in hand and sat on a chair at the kitchen table across from Meredith.

"I apologize," Phyllis said. "Didn't mean to run out on you."

"I hope I'm not interrupting," Meredith said.

"No, no. I silenced my phone to meditate and regroup," she said, lowering her gaze. Her voice quavered as hot tears stung her eyes and spilled down her face. "I feel overwhelmed. Randy's probation issues and community service is still unresolved. Bills need to be paid. I—I needed a quiet moment to reflect. I wondered if anyone loved me, whether God still loves me."

Meredith pushed her coffee cup aside and faced Phyllis directly. "God still loves you! His loving arms are outreached to you."

At Meredith's remarks, Phyllis raised her head and began to release the weight she'd been carrying by pouring out the details of Randy's situation. "The judge gave him a fine that we've already paid but he gave Randy two stipulations. First, *he* has to pay the fine. He's been ordered to get a job for the summer and turn the money over to me until it's paid back. When I hand in his pay stubs and voucher that he's paid the fine, then his earnings from then on are his."

"That sounds great! Randy's sixteen, he needs to learn to work."

"I know. I've never asked him to but—"

"*But* he will now," Meredith added. "He'll still have plenty of time to enjoy the summer and have fun."

"Randy has to do forty hours of community work. The judge said something about how it would perhaps satisfy his stipulations if it is a conflict in school, but he said Randy must immediately begin working the required hours."

"Our church has teen service projects where the kids volunteer their time at the church and in the community. If he does well enough, he might find a paying job with the church in one of the auxiliaries. They always need help with outside projects. You can make an appointment with Pastor McKnight tomorrow. At least Randy will be busy using his time helping others and getting together with some of the church teens. It's perfect."

"Thanks for listening and for being a great friend. I don't want to talk about this with everyone. I'm sure you understand."

"That's what friends are for, Phyll. Of course I understand." Meredith laid a soft hand over Phyllis. "How about we pray for this concern?"

Phyllis agreed, and Meredith began the prayer. She took a Bible out of her strapped leather purse and opened it to a passage in 2 Corinthians. Her eyes swept over the passages and then began to read:

> *My grace is sufficient for you, for my power is made perfect in weakness.* (2 Corinthians 12:9 NIV)

> *Because of the extravagance of those revelations, and so I wouldn't get a big head, I was given the gift of a handicap to keep me in constant touch with my limitations. Satan's angel did his best to get me down; what he in fact did was push me to my knees. No danger then of walking around high and mighty! At first I didn't think of it as a gift, and begged God to remove it. Three times I did that, and then he told me, My grace is enough; it's all you need. My strength comes into its own in your weakness. Once I heard that, I was glad to let it happen. I quit focusing on the handicap and began appreciating the gift. It was a case of Christ's strength moving in on my weakness. Now I take limitations in stride, and with good cheer, these limitations that*

cut me down to size—abuse, accidents, opposition, bad breaks. I just let Christ take over! And so the weaker I get, the stronger I become. (2 Corinthians 12:7-10 MSG)

"God wants you to exchange your weakness for His strength. It's a fair exchange," Meredith said. "God's loving arms are outstretched to you," Meredith repeatedly assured Phyllis. After the brief prayer, she stood up to leave.

Later, Phyllis massaged the tension in her neck as she settled down at the glass kitchen table and let the words wash over her like a cool refreshing shower.

CHAPTER 7

PHYLLIS RESTED ON a cushioned stool at the granite-topped island in the middle of the kitchen. Its sprinkling of tiny tan-colored specks reminded her of pebbles on a sandy beach. Except for the hum of the refrigerator, the house was quiet. She watched Randy get on the school bus and had already taken Chrissie to day care.

Around 7:30 a.m., she called Pastor McKnight's office. His secretary, Mrs. Bradley, answered the phone. "Good morning! Mrs. Bradley speaking. How may I help you?"

Phyllis greeted the secretary with high expectations of achieving her goal for Randy. "Would it be possible for me to make an appointment with Pastor McKnight this *morning*?" Phyllis asked, emphasizing the word *morning*.

"Just a moment please, I'll check his schedule for today." After a few minutes, Mrs. Bradley confirmed that a morning appointment was available (to her surprise).

"That's great!" The words flew out of Phyllis's mouth. "What time please?"

"Pastor McKnight starts his day early. His first appointment begins at eight. Will nine o'clock work for you?"

"Perfect timing!" Phyllis beamed a broad smile that showed her dimpled cheeks.

"We'll see you at nine," said Mrs. Bradley. "Pastor McKnight keeps a busy schedule. Please let us know if you decide to cancel for any reason."

Later at around eight o'clock, she called Rylander's office number to asked for a couple of hours off to get to her appointment with Pastor McKnight.

"Good morning, this is Rylander."

"Hello," Phyllis greeted him and requested approval for paid leave for a couple of hours.

"Approved, but a staff's meeting scheduled for three. Don't miss it!"

"Thanks," Phyllis said waiving a dismissive hand at his dogmatic tone.

As her boss hang up, a sparkle came into her eyes. *So far, so good,* she thought. She'd have plenty of time to meet with Pastor McKnight and make it to work on time for the mandatory staff meeting.

A cell phone rang above the clamor of her mind. The familiar ringtone was Meredith's.

"Tonight we're discussing plans for the Walkabout and Waterfront Faire. Can you come?"

"Where?" asked Phyllis.

"My place, seven o'clock."

"Sure, see you then. Oh, by the way, I have an appointment with Pastor McKnight. I'm meeting him in an hour."

"Great! Keep your chin up. I'll see you tonight," Meredith said.

Phyllis remembered last year's event. Grayson volunteered as a tour guide dressed in a colonial costume and guided tourists through the scenic gardens. Chrissie had gotten a kick out of seeing her dad dressed in the whacky outfit. It would be different this year. For one, there would be no Grayson.

The grandfather clock in the living room chimed eight thirty. Phyllis scampered upstairs to her bedroom closet and slipped into an orange floral dress with an orange bolero jacket. Then she swept her hair back into a roll and fingered a single auburn strand that curled down the side of her face. Cream-colored shoes and a matching purse completed her trendy outfit. Phyllis eyed her form in the mirror and scurried out of the house with the purse slung over her shoulder. The orange color accentuated her brown eyes that sparkled against her honey-brown complexion.

Energetic and *upbeat* were two words that she hadn't used to describe her emotions in a long time. This morning was different. Could it be the verse that Meredith read from the Bible on last night? The words echoed in her mind. *It was a case of Christ's strength moving in on my weakness. Now I take my limitations in stride and with good cheer. These limitations that cut me down to size—abuse, accidents, opposition, and bad breaks. I just let Christ take over. So the weaker I get, the stronger I become.* She wanted to become strong and get past her current situation. To be a good mother for Randy and Chrissie.

A while later, near the intersection of Union Street, the large stone church loomed in front of her. Crisp morning air hit her face, and the sweet chirp of red robins on a nearby maple uplifted her spirits. Her feet glided with ease up the stone steps at a leisurely pace. A historical marker etched in the cornerstone proclaimed the St. Mark's Church of Schenectady as one of the oldest landmarks in the city. Phyllis entered the building through its double oak doors. Inside, she noticed rosette windows in the front and along the back of the sanctuary. Pastor McKnight's office was located in the rear, a few steps from the main entrance. Inspirational plaques lined the hallway. The quiet atmosphere seemed to welcome her.

"Hello, Mrs. Whitmore," Pastor McKnight said, a friendly smile spread across his face as he extended his right hand for a firm but gentle handshake. He towered over Phyllis.

"Good morning," she said, stepping forward and warmly clasping his extended hand. Phyllis noticed a hint of gray peeking from under ebony sideburns on his medium frame.

"Please, come in."

She strode into his office and took a seat in a Queen Ann chair facing him. A large Bible lay on his desk with yellow highlights on an open page. A quick glance gave her a full view of the spacious office that contained an small but impressive library.

"How may I assist you?" he asked.

Phyllis explained that Randy was on probation and needed to complete forty hours of community service right away. He must also attend truancy classes for a month to fulfill his probation requirements. For several minutes, she talked about her concerns for Randy and her frustration as a single parent.

Pastor McKnight stroked his stub of a gray beard, a habit of his when he focused intently. He scribbled a name and a phone number on a Post-it Note and gave it to Phyllis. "Call Jerry Allensworth. He and his wife oversee our youth programs, I'm sure they can help you. They might be able to get Randy started as early as next week."

After their brief meeting, Pastor McKnight prayed with Phyllis. She rose from her chair to leave and offered her hand in a grateful handshake. Pastor McKnight shook her hand and informed her to call him if he could further assist her. "You and your family are welcomed to worship with us anytime. We have services on Wednesday and Sundays. Come anytime. We hope to see you soon."

"Thank you, I'd love to," Phyllis remarked and nodded in a friendly gesture. She left relieved but anxious for Randy to begin community service, hopefully the next week. It was an answer to prayer and a relief to her anxiety.

* * *

As Phyllis pulled the Lexus into her assigned parking space at work, she arrived a half hour earlier than she originally thought. Strolling to the office, she noticed the usual atmosphere. Lil and her coworkers were working like an army of ants, preparing for the three o'clock meeting with Rylander.

At 2:59 p.m. sharp, Rylander began the staff meeting. The staff was expected to be present a few minutes before the scheduled time. "Let's not waste any time. During our last staff meeting, you were given assignments. Whitmore, let's start with your report first," Rylander said, running his hand through his hair and leaning back on his chair.

Phyllis swiveled her chair to directly face him. "The financial packets have been turned over to our attorneys. They are reviewing them and investigating the various legalities involved."

"When do you expect them to get back with you?"

"In a couple of days."

"Great!" Rylander sent her a wink of approval. His hand smoothed the cranberry-colored silk tie hanging neatly over his black slacks. Louis Van Niemen made his report next, then Kurt Wilson, and followed by James Rogers. "Good job, everyone, but I have a bit of bad news," Rylander announced. "We are about to kick into high gear. We may have to work overtime. I know how you all feel about OT, but bite the bullet." He glanced around the conference table.

Louis Van Niemen arched an eyebrow and his jaw fell open. Except Phyllis, everyone adopted a similar expression. Her face remained placid, unchanged. She welcomed the overtime opportunity, especially since Grayson had left and taken a big chunk of their money with him, wiping out the bank account. Now she was facing a delinquent mortgage. Gratitude reign in her spirit.

"Okay, that's all for now," Rylander said, dismissing the meeting.

Phyllis and the other staff returned to their desks as their boss rummaged through some papers in front him. Phyllis worked diligently, making a call to the attorneys for new updates on the project. After work, Phyllis drove straight to Lil Tots. It bustled with parents streaming in and out of the building like shoppers hustling to buy last-minute Christmas gifts.

"I'm hungry, Mommy!" Chrissie whined insistently, strapped in her seat in the back of the car. Phyllis eyed the looming yellow arch ahead and swung into McDonald's. She decided to order a drive-through meal because of the meeting at Meredith's that night. The aroma of french fries and cheeseburgers soon filled the car.

At home, Randy was already settled in his room with music lulling his ears. Phyllis set the bag of food on the kitchen island and yelled upstairs for him to come down and eat. A few seconds later, Randy bolted down the stairs and placed his cell phone on the kitchen counter long enough to grab two cheeseburgers, pile some fries on his plate, and pop open a can of soda. He quickly snatched his phone and bounded up the stairs to his room, all the while yapping to Kerry Mitterson on his cell phone.

* * *

A tiny smile played at the corners of Meredith's mouth. She looked forward to hosting the Walkabout meeting and doing it in her usual way with her famous goodies—an assortment of chocolate chip, oatmeal raisin, mint chocolate, and peanut butter cookies all neatly arranged on a silver serving tray. The cookies would be set in the middle of the coffee table next to a tall green vase filled with freshly cut lilies. No one could refuse the taste and delicious aroma of those cookies hot out of the over.

Phyllis leaned back in her chair and joined Charla Myerson and Melissa Guvenstaf who were nibbling one of their favorite cookies. No one came to Meredith's home, especially on an occasion like tonight, without sampling her freshly baked delicacies.

"Thanks for coming," said Mrs. Creighton, shifting her plus-sized frame on the large chocolate-brown sofa. It was the same color as her eyes, which complimented her short, curly brunette hair with a hint of silver around the edges. "I won't keep you long," she promised in a raspy voice, "but with our annual Stockade Walkabout only a month away, we need to finalize plans to make this event a greater success than last year's. We have two new highlights this year. Tourist and the town folks will have the opportunity to tour an active archaeological dig on Front Street and also a treasure hunt. First, we need to set up our website so people can buy tickets online. Who can do that?"

"I will," Melissa Guvenstaf said. She pushed her glasses up on her freckled nose and tucked a strand of reddish-brown hair behind her ear.

"Who'll volunteer to contact the entertainers?"

Charla's hand shot up while she held a chocolate chip cookie in the other. "I will," she said eagerly. Music and entertainment was right up her alley.

"Will anyone volunteer to organize the home and church tours? Eleven Stocktadians will open their doors this year. As always, we'll need several tour guides. Phyllis, how about your husband? He did an excellent job last year. Would you ask him to help us again?"

Phyllis swallowed hard, pleased that her voice was steady when she spoke. "I won't be able to do that. We're divorced," she replied

LIVING SANE IN A CRAZY WORLD

shamefully, lowering her gaze to the coffee table as she grappled with the mood of the room.

"I'm sorry, Phyllis dear." She rose from her seat and ambled over to Phyllis to give her a bear-hug. Mrs. Ruthie Creighton was the motherly type, a gentle and kind lady. Charla and Melissa cocked their heads and slanted a sideways glance at each other. "You mustn't let anything stop you from going on with your life. Life happens!" said Mrs. Creighton as she continued to hold Phyllis.

Phyllis pretended to look for something in her purse, trying hard to maintain her composure. She was not ready for their pity yet appreciated their kindness.

Ruthie Creighton continued her discussion, and the meeting gained momentum. A short while later, she wrapped it up. "Ladies, I believe we've covered all of our grounds. Thanks for your support and for all of your hard work. Now let's hop to it!"

On her way home, Phyllis' cell phone hummed in her purse. She dug it out.

Zel Palmer, one of her classmates from Albany, New York, was calling. "Hello, Phyllis. Good news! Our class reunion is coming up. I'm heading up the planning committee. Lydia, Georgette, and I are coming to Schenectady a week early next month to help me. We hoped you'd join us."

"You're late starting, aren't you?" Phyllis asked.

"Yeah, yeah, yeah. My middle name is *still* procrastination, but I get the job done. That's all that matters," Zel chuckled, signaling the truth about her delay in getting things accomplished.

"Sounds great!" Phyllis said, thinking it was not a good time to entertain anyone in her frame of mind and situation. "I can't wait to see you," she said in an effort to get rid of Zel.

* * *

A month passed like a blur. The day had finally arrived and the Waterfront and Walkabout Faire was in full swing. Although extreme temperatures had become a daily occurrence, the late June heat was not a problem today. Not even for the petunias, marigolds and some of the other flowers that splashed various colors that recently began to wilt under the persistent heat. Tourist and the town folks paraded through the streets in droves. No one seemed to mind the warm temperature. Carriage rides drawn by snow-white horses clopped on the asphalt under an enormous white banner with bold black letters that read, "The 44th Annual Stockade Walkabout." It stretched across the corner of Front and Ferry Streets.

A crowd of teenagers gathered at the circular plaza around the statute of Lawrence chattering and singing along with the music. The famous Indian statute stood upright surrounded by a white circular fence and served as a popular gathering place. Crowds of teens gathered to hear the Union College Jazz Band filling the air with the latest hits propped on a platform under a giant oak tree. Even the Mohawk River had its share of activity. An inbound boat chugged its way over the calm surface.

A warm breeze stirred across the Mohawk River and ruffled Phyllis' curly locks. She turned her face away from direct sunlight as she and Chrissie marched along Front Street. She did not want to come to the Walkabout Faire today. In the past, like most Schnectadians, the event was second only to Christmas, being a cross between a carnival and old-fashioned community picnic. Last year, she and Grayson walked hand-in-hand. This year, she and Chrissie walked hand-in-hand. *If forget ifs*, she thought. She felt nostalgic but decided it was too nice a day to feel blue.

Chrissie spotted a teddy bear display ahead of them. "Get teddy bear, Mommy." She wrestled her hand out of Phyllis' grip and raced to the sidewalk booth. The teddy bear stand sat between the quilt and the spinning wheel in front of Bill Freedman's ice cream shop. Phyllis caught up with Chrissie and gently reprimanded her to not take off like that again.

"Hello, young lady. Which bear do you want?"

Chrissie pointed at a deep purple bear with the glassy button eyes. Phyllis handed the man the money. The potbellied vendor handed Chrissie the bear and thanked Phyllis for her business. Chrissie immediately gave the bear a hug and clung to it possessively. It was then that Phyllis observed another parent scolding her child.

"No, you cannot have two teddies," the mother ranted while holding her toddler's hand.

The child leaned backward, kicking and crying out loud while holding the teddy under his arms. He was throwing a tantrum because he could not have his way. The cone of strawberry ice cream was rapidly melting under the sweltering heat in his other hand. Phyllis attempted a smile that dispelled the discouragement she felt.

Displays were erected on all of the street corners. One display that captivated some of the hunters was the display that showed the progression of bullets. Hunters flocked to this display.

"Hey!" shouted Kyle Sumrall, eyeing Randy and Kerry Mitterson strutting and chattering in front of him with their hands clasped as they stood eating globs of the pastel spun sugar by the facing the cotton candy machine.

Hearing a familiar voice echoing behind him, Randy turned on his heel and saw Kyle Sumrall and Lela Everette munching on Italian sausages on a stick. They raced to each other's side. Conversation buzzed among them. Soon they lost themselves in the crowd, joining in the fun and excitement of the fair.

Phyllis wiped the sweat on her forehead with the palm of her hand as she and Chrissie moved aimlessly through the crowd. She enjoyed a double scoop of chocolate ice cream.

A drunk almost toppled her over as he slung an unauthorized beer can at another drunk close to where she and Chrissie were walking. "Hit me agin!" the drunk hollered, emptying a bottle up to his mouth and staggering three steps backward and two steps forward.

"Why you yeller, lemme alone," the other drunk shrieked at the top of his voice.

Even Boxcar Willie and the other drunk celebrated the annual Stockade Walkabout.

"Who dat, Mommy?" Chrissie tugged at her Mom's Capri pants, questioning the drunks' behavior.

"Oh, just someone misbehaving, precious," said Phyllis.

Schenectady was a hodgepodge of activity with folks strolling in and out of historic homes filled with invigorating scents, including the spicy aroma of Italian sausage and hot dogs roasting on the grill side by side and homemade jams and jellies from vendors that lined the crowded streets. Tour guides dressed in colonial outfits sauntered up Front Street with tourist and town people snaking around corners, snapping photographs of flowering gardens on Ferry Street.

Phyllis spotted Meredith striding toward her. "I made it." Meredith told Phyllis that she'd join her after she ran some errands.

Above the ruckus of the crowd, Phyllis heard the shrill of a whistle pierce the air. She and Meredith turned in that direction. Out of nowhere, two teenage boys darted past Phyllis, almost knocking her and Chrissie around. *Is this knock-me-down day?* she wondered. *First the drunks, now the disobedient teens?* A security guard was in hot pursuit, pointing his index finger and yelling at them to scram. The teens were quicker on their feet and outran the guard. They sped away, chuckling mischievously.

Meredith helped Phyllis straighten and gain her composure. Phyllis' gaze drifted over the crowd. Then her eyes widened. She stood frozen in her position. She gasped and then cupped her mouth with both hands. "Phyllis, is there something wrong?" Meredith asked. She followed Phyllis' gaze.

Was her eyes deceiving her? Was that her ex-husband Grayson… with Birdie? Grayson's warm smile had Birdie's full attention Phyllis thought she saw him put his arms around Birdie's shoulders. The short ebony hair and the giggle was Birdie's all right. She giggled like a kid at Ringling Brothers' clown performance. She saw them disappear into the crowd. Tears filled her eyes, which she angrily swiped away with the back of her hand.

Meredith could see the obvious hurt and pain in her friend's face. "You'll be all right," she said, patting Phyllis on the shoulder. "I'm sorry I won't be able to stay. I'm going to buy some homemade jams and jellies then I must leave. I'll talk to you later." Meredith gave Phyllis a loving embrace. "Be good, sweetie pie," she told Chrissie, stoking her chin before she left.

Olivia, Birdie's identical twin sister, recognized Grayson and thought she'd catch up on old times with her former classmate. Birdie promised Olivia she'd join her at the Walkabout Faire later after catching a few more hours of sleep. She was no early bird. Unlike Birdie,

Olivia was genuine and sincere. Apart from their resemblance, they were complete opposites.

Chrissie tugged at her mom's legs, this time eyeing a hotdog stand two feet away. Walking in a daze, Phyllis meandered over to the booth and bought her a hotdog.

Only a few feet further away, Georgette took a bite out of a mustard-covered corn dog when she spotted Phyllis at the hotdog stand with Chrissie. She and Zel both ran to them, their arms flailing in the air, straight into Phyllis' arms. Girly screams sailed through the air like kids racing to a playground at recess.

"Hello, Phyllis. I haven't seen you in ages," Georgette said, giving her a tight embrace.

Zel reached down to Chrissie with her long hair falling over her shoulders. "My, aren't you a cutie!" She affectionately pinched Chrissie's cheeks. Chrissie clung to Phyllis, not wanting to be disturbed as she ate her hot dog.

Phyllis returned the hug but the distraction of the image of Grayson and Birdie still hung heavily in her mind. She hadn't seen Georgette in five years, but today she'd rather not see her or Zel. She only stayed at the fair for Chrissie's sake, but her heart was not in it anymore.

"I'm dying to go on the treasure hunt," Zel said. "C'mon, let's all go!"

Phyllis wanted to save face and told them it was almost nap time for Chrissie and that she'd hang out with them later. The image of Grayson and Birdie still upset her.

CHAPTER 8

PHYLLIS HEADED HOME, leaving the hustle and bustle of the fair behind. She wished that she could leave her unsettled emotions behind as well. The late afternoon sun streaked across the river, and the setting sun painted the sky with rose, emerald, and gold hues. Looking out of the window of the car, she noticed the rippling waves that played and danced along the edges of the Mohawk like children frolicking in the street. The playful waves calmed her. Leaning forward against the steering wheel, she turned on the radio and found a light jazz station, leaving it low volume. The soft music lulled her like a sleeping baby until the tension from earlier eased.

Paying the bills crossed her mind. It's not something you normally forget, but since Grayson left, she had been too busy to organize and pay them with the limited amount of funds left. The divorce, upkeep of the house, Randy's probation, raising a toddler, caring for a dog, and working a full-time job weighed on her spirits like weights on a scale. Life overwhelmed her. This evening, however, taking care of the delinquent mortgage was top priority. Normally, handling the finances would frustrate her. Grayson took care of the bills and things related to finances.

Chrissie had fallen asleep in the car before they arrived home. Phyllis dressed her and put her in bed, smothering her cheeks with gentle kisses. Randy hadn't called or came home yet. Undoubtedly, he was somewhere lollygagging with Kerry Mitterson who was probably wrapped around him like a snake on a pole.

A shower and a couple hours later, with Champion trotting besides her, Phyllis turned on the laptop on the desk in her bedroom and settled herself to focus on the bills. She drew in a lengthy breath. Deep creases furrowed her forehead as she attentively read the contents of each envelope. She scribbled a list of bills on a writing pad and opened an spreadsheet to perform the calculations. Phyllis typed the figures from the bills on the spreadsheet before hitting the sigma function key that totaled the large amount needed to pay off all of the bills.

"America the Beautiful" chimed loudly on her cell phone and interrupted her thoughts.

"I thought I'd call and check on you after today's scene. Are you okay?" Meredith asked in a concerned voice on the other end.

"Yes, yes, I'm okay."

"Do you need anything?"

"No, thanks."

"Are you sure Phyllis?"

"Yes, I'm sure," Phyllis assured Meredith and promised to call again soon before she hung up the phone.

Her eyes rested on the pile of bills cluttered in the corner of the desk. Since Grayson left, she carelessly tossed them on the desk. Her lean fingers quickly shuffled through the disorganized stack when she focused on the certified letter labeled "THIRD NOTICE" from Fidelity of Schenectady. The bold words glared at her like the eyes of a bull charging a matador. "Payment must be received immediately to avoid foreclosure." An empty bank account and two weeks away from her next payday made the situation crucial. Fear spiraled in Phyllis' mind. She massaged her temples to ease the pressure. How was she going to get the extra funds she desperately needed for the mortgage? Payment was due now! She had never known shortage, except for the time that her mother could no longer take care of her any longer after her dad died and she had to live with her grandmother. Times were hard, but things worked out before long. She couldn't lose the house now. How could Grayson do this to her? To Randy and to Chrissie?

After a long while, a light bulb came on. *Overtime!* Hadn't Rylander informed the staff that the Fontnel project was about to kick into high gear and that he had approved overtime funds to work on the project? Why didn't she think of this before? She'd earn extra money by working as many overtime hours as she could. She smiled in relief.

Champion let out a wide yawn and nuzzled against her legs. "Okay, time for bed," Phyllis said, gazing into his drowsy eyes. She took him in her arms and stroked his shaggy coat while making her way to his bed downstairs. Afterward, Phyllis scurried back to her calculations.

Her mind traveled back to the incident at the Walkabout Faire with Grayson and Birdie. She tried to let it go, but it wouldn't let go of her. She recalled when she was six years old and lived with her grandmother, Maggie Sullivan. "Lord, let your hand become my help," Granny often prayed whenever she encountered difficult situations. It seemed she lifted up that prayer daily to help her through tough times. Phyllis now found herself whispering the same prayer. Yanking the phone from the receiver, she dialed Granny's number. She quickly hung up before Granny could answer. She needed to tell her about the divorce but couldn't force herself to tell her *now.* Admitting defeat, she punched her grandmother's number into her cell phone.

"Hello, sweetie," Granny answered, recognizing the familiar phone number on her caller ID. "How are you on this lovely evening?" she asked Phyllis affectionately.

"I'm...I'm fine," she managed to say before she burst out in uncontrollable tears.

"Now, now, sweetie. I knew something was wrong, I sensed it in your voice. You should know your granny well enough by now. You can't hide anything from me that the Lord shows me." Maggie Sullivan always had an uncanny way of knowing and sensing things, especially where Phyllis was concerned. "Why the tears? Tell me all about it."

Phyllis reclined in the chair and related the whole story about the foreclosure and seeing Grayson with Birdie.

"Why that's awful! The scumbag!" Granny huffed in her most unpleasant tone. "Hmm, I see. Let me help you, sweetie," Granny said in a loving and caring manner. I'll just put a check in the mail to you tomorrow."

"No, we're fine," Phyllis assured her. "I just needed to hear your voice tonight."

"Sweetie," she said, in a just-listen-to-me voice, "you have a beautiful family. God is faithful to help those who call on Him for guidance and provision. Visit me soon, bring the children. I want to see you all."

"I'll bring them soon."

"Promise?"

"Promise," Phyllis said.

"I know you're hurt, but God has promised that all things work together for our good, even the painful things. We'll just pray for Grayson," Granny said before she and Phyllis said their farewells.

Phyllis drew in a long breath as her grandmother's consoling words settled over her. She decided that she would visit Granny soon after her life quieted down. A shrill noise from the dryer rang throughout the house, indicating the end of the cycle. She went downstairs to the laundry room.

* * *

Loud chatter floated on the air in Saint Mark's Church of Schenectady's youth center. Randy and Roberto McClellan walked toward the youth center.

"The girls are cool and fine," said Roberto McClellan, slapping Randy on the back as they cornered the building. "C'mon, you'll see."

This piqued Randy's interest even more that he picked up his pace. Randy's bow-legged friend stood a few feet shorter than his own six-foot frame. Roberto gazed up at Randy with a mischievous grin as they walked up to the church, talking about the girls. Randy returned his gaze with the same mischievous grin. The room near the atrium buzzed with noise as one rambunctious teens squawked to another. The excitement in the room reminded Randy of the roar of Schenectady High School's football team when they played against Anderson High, their local rival team. A few of the teens munched on chips and sipped sodas that had been served by a group of youth volunteers.

"Hello, everyone. Let's welcome Randy Whitmore. He's joining our youth group and will also be working with Mr. Littleton on the Youth for Tomorrow project," Jerry Allensworth announced. "I'm proud to be your director and thrilled to see that our group is growing. C'mon, let's make Randy feel at home." Mr. Allensworth cheered the group on with his resonant clapping to demonstrate his enthusiastic welcome. The group hushed to a still at his authority. "Please introduce yourselves. Clayton, let's start with you."

Clayton playfully spun around on a stool, displaying a full set of pearly teeth. Aida Finn sat next to him near the oak-paneled wall. "What's up?" Clayton introduced himself to Randy. Aida followed.

Ten minutes later, after everyone had made their introductions, Mr. Allensowrth faced Randy. "Tell us about yourself, Randy," he said, smiling warmly.

Randy scanned the crowd, flipping a long braid over his broad shoulder. "What's up?" he asked rhetorically. He then told them his school's name and home address, which was all he intended to share. He felt a little out of place in the mist of twenty "churchy" kids. He wanted try to worm his way out of this. Roberto McClelland was the only reason he came tonight. He said the girls were *cool* and *fine*. He already worked fervently, thanks to his mom. He was able to complete half of his community service hours, working on the youth project. Now it seemed he'd have to finish without the company of Roberto. Randy arched a brow and sighed. The only thing he wanted to do was leave.

"Thanks everyone," Mr. Allensworth booming voice resounded. "Okay, it's time to work on your group projects. Randy, you'll work with group number three. Clayton, I need the larger boxes filled first. I've assigned Frank and Adam to help you. Let me know when you're done, I'll give you further instructions then."

"Yes, sir," Clayton replied. "Will do."

Randy sat across the table from Toby McPhie and Bobbie Hillrodden who had been in the program for several months. He ambled to the table and kept his gaze lowered. He caught a fresh whiff of gardenia and raised his head, meeting Sarah Rose's hazel eyes staring into his own. A million butterflies flitted in his stomach. His eyes was fixed on hers for what seemed like a lifetime as she eased in a chair across for the table opposite of him.

"Randy, would you like to begin our activity tonight?" asked Mr. Allensworth, focusing in Randy's direction.

"Yes...yes, sir," Randy stammered when someone eventually poked his elbow and brought him back to reality. Roberto was right about the girls. He agreed completely that the girls were cool—at least Sarah Rose seemed all right.

* * *

Phyllis pulled the tangled bedsheets and other linens from the dryer and dropped them into the laundry basket to fold upstairs later. The doorbell rang repeatedly before she could determine the caller, wondering who could be at her door. For a brief moment, she remembered Grayson walking through the door with his briefcase in hand and Chrissie running into his embrace. The doorbell chimed loudly once more, bringing her back to reality. She raced from the laundry room to the front door. Phyllis peeked through the peephole, flinched, and blew out an exasperated breath. She moved her head from side to side and then opened the door.

"Hello, Little Sis," Wylie, her brother, greeted Phyllis. An impish grin cornered his mouth as his lanky frame stumbled over the threshold when Phyllis opened the door wider. He extended his outreached arms to encircle her with a bear hug, his breath reeking of alcohol and tobacco.

"What do you want, Wylie?" she asked, rubbing the bridge of her nose with the palm of her hand. She frowned and put a hand on her hip. His unstable and irresponsible life flashed before her in a fraction of a moment. She stood in the doorway, staring into his shifty brown eyes. "What's up, Wylie?" Phyllis asked again, her head leaning on the inside of the door.

"Oscar and I had a tiff. I just need a place to stay for a couple of months. I was wondering if I could bring my things over, say tomorrow night?" Phyllis poked an index finger into his chest and mouthed the words "Get a job." "I'm trying to snag a job. C'mon, Sis," he pleaded, stumbling all over.

George and Kevin refused to deal with Wylie and his careless lifestyle. As the youngest brother, Oscar's quiet and nonsensical personality stood out above Wylie and the other brothers. Phyllis felt convinced that Wylie was probably acting out so Oscar sent him packing.

"Where's my sugar cakes?" he affectionately referred to Chrissie. Where's—what's his name?"

Maybe it was the alcohol, but he could never remember Grayson's name. She shushed him before he could awaken Chrissie. "She's sound asleep," Phyllis answered, sidestepping his question about Grayson. "It's nice seeing you, but it's time for you to leave now."

Wylie laughed, making the skin around his eyes crinkle. "You think I'm drunk, but I'm not."

"That's a moot point, Wylie." Drunk or not, she didn't want him bothering her, especially now.

She slammed the door shut, unconcerned about the noise, and marched to the den ahead of Wylie who stumbled behind her. He reached the sofa and fell heavily on it. He snored as soon as his head touched the plush leather. Phyllis ambled to the linen closet, grabbed a blanket from the shelf, and plumped up a pillow. She threw it over Wylie.

"Good night," Phyllis said, looking down at him knocked out on the sofa, his mouth wide open and snoring loudly. "I'll see you off tomorrow." She stormed off, nostrils flaring that he had the nerve to barge in on her now.

She checked on Chrissie a couple of times before she slipped into the shower. The cool water invigorated her body and mind. Had it not been for Wylie's intrusion, the evening would have ended on a happier note. Phyllis dried off, slathered lotion on her body, and slipped into a pair of silky ice-blue pajamas. He padded downstairs to the kitchen to make a cup of coffee. Phillis froze at the rustling of the key in the lock.

Randy stepped into the den, his cell phone glued to his ears as usual. "Hi, Mom." Immediately, he whispered into his phone, "I'll call you back later."

"Where have you been?"

"I was at *that* church with all those *churchy* kids," Randy responded, staring Phyllis directly in the eyes. He waited for her to lower the boom. She was always mad about something concerning him. *No wonder Dad left. It was all her fault*, Randy thought.

Phyllis smiled, recalling what Pastor McKnight said about Randy starting his community service at Saint Mark's this week. She hugged him and gave him an affectionate pat on the back. *What a relief*, she thought. Randy did something right for once. "Oh, Uncle Wylie is sprawled on the sofa. He's drunk. I'm sure a stampede of frightened elephants couldn't wake him up but keep your music low. Good night, Randy."

"Good night, Mom," Randy said and shot across the room to the refrigerator.

CHAPTER 9

"FILE THESE WITH the other documents," Rylander ordered, leaning over Lil's desk at the office. A few of the numerous folders propped under his arms toppled on Lil's desk.

She extended a slender hand to grab the other manila folders before they collided with other piles of documents on her workstation. She gave him a you're trying-to-do-too-much look with her usual smile.

"Thanks, Lil," Rylander said. He sent her a broad smile, which was not his usual demeanor, before he sprinted to his office on the other side of the room.

The contract for the Fontnel project had been finalized and yielded fruit after weeks of much hard work. Worth millions, obtaining this contract was the business deal that every major company in Schenectady sought after. The Fontnel project now officially belonged to Monterey and Cleary. The company won big. William Barrett Rylander paraded around like a multimillion-dollar-lottery winner ten times over. Things were on a roll. Staff buzzed nonstop around the office like Christmas shoppers at a 75-percent-off sale at Macy's. Rylander breezed into the conference room, whistling his favorite tune and strutting to the coffee nook in the corner. With thoughts of sweet victory parading across his mind, he grabbed a large mug, filled it to the brim, gulped the dark brew down, and carried it to his glossy cherrywood table. He plopped the armful of documents down on the head of the table. Dressed in an impeccable gray pinstripe suit, Rylander's style spoke volumes about his good taste in clothes.

Phyllis strode into the conference room still rehearsing plans in her mind to discuss working extra hours with Rylander. She decided to wait until after their staff meeting. Did she feel apprehensive? *Not at all*, she thought. Rylander already told the staff to work overtime. Although the contract had been officially awarded, there were still documents to be finalized that could necessitate working a few extra hours. For once, she felt her prayers had been answered and things seemed to be going her way.

The office meeting ended on a high note. The staff left chatting and exchanging office jargon as they scattered to their separate work areas. At the end of the workday, Phyllis gathered up notepad and pen and made a beeline for Rylander who was still seated at the conference table. "Rylander, excuse me," she began. "I'll be working late tonight." Silence. Rylander's eyes lingered on Phyllis for what seemed like eternity, butterflies fluttered in her stomach. She felt uneasy at his intense stare, being alone with him in the large empty room. Phyllis narrowed her eyes and returned his stare with a puzzled look. Thinking fast, she restrained herself from placing a hand on her hip, her typical expression of her anger or frustration.

Rylander cleared his throat with a deep cough. "Yeah, that's fine." He returned to the papers sprawled on the table.

"Thanks." Phyllis tore out of the conference room to her desk where she focused steadily on her job for the next three hours.

Her thoughts wandered for a moment. *Where is Lil?* Working late was her normal routine. *Why didn't some of the other staff worked this evening?* Van Nieman and Robert Wilson were both financially secure to her knowledge. While money was no issue for either of them, Rylander mandated everybody work overtime. No excuses, he said. Tonight she welcomed the company of anyone rather than be alone with him. *Maybe they had medical or dental appointments. Maybe soccer game with the kids or maybe something else.*

Eight o'clock came at a snail's pace. She did not linger when the hands on the clock pointed at the hour. She didn't want to spend one minute with Rylander in the office more than she had to. After finishing her work quickly, she straightened her desk and left. Driving home that night, Phyllis' thoughts were all over the place. *Maybe overtime was not a good idea*, she mused.

Her cell phone buzzed, interrupting her thoughts. "Hello?" Phyllis answered, somewhat relieved to be distracted of her chaotic thoughts.

"Hi, Mom. Roberto and his dad picked me up for community service tonight," her son said.

"That's great, Randy." She smiled.

"See ya later, Mom."

"Sure. Be good, son."

Phyllis tapped the red button on her cell phone and ended Randy's call. A smile tugged at the corner of her mouth as she sped up Washington Street, tightly gripping the steering wheel. She was grateful that she called Meredith who agreed to pick Chrissie up from day care and keep her until she could pick her up after work. Meredith Hightower was more than a friend, she was a true sister.

She blinked as thoughts of Rylander's antics shot across her mind. She didn't feel comfortable with him now. He had never been disrespectful with her before. *What was going on in his mind now?* she wondered. *Could it be that the Fontnel project had given him a big head?* Whatever the reason, it was another hurdle on her obstacle course of life.

Phyllis let out a deep breath and steered the Lexus down Washington Street for a few more blocks. Half an hour later at 8:30 p.m., she parked the car in front of Meredith's house, raced to the door, and rang the doorbell. Phyllis announced herself loudly as she rang the doorbell so Meredith could easily recognize her. Meredith flung the door open and stepped aside with her usual beaming smile. Phyllis waved hello to her and stepped through the doorway of the den. Pearly teeth beamed across her face as she crouched to the floor, watching Chrissie leap from the leather sofa.

Arms flailing in the air, Chrissie raced into her mom's arms. "Mommy, Mommy!"

"Hi, sweetie pie." Phyllis ruffled her thick ebony curls and smothered Chrissie in warm kisses and tender hugs. She stood on her feet and gave Meredith a huge bear-hug. "Thanks a zillion!" After much thanks, they left Meredith waving good-bye in the doorway.

The day had been hectic. Rylander's antics still lingered on her mind. His actions were unprecedented and puzzling. Thoughts of reaching her home in the stockade district relaxed her mind. Like the nearby Mohawk, she intended to handle the twists and turns of her life. It was only a question of when.

Phyllis sped into the driveway, eager to enter the house and call it a day. She had only one plan tonight, make a quick snack, dress Chrissie for bed, and crawl into her own bed as fast as she could. In a flash, she parked the car and lifted Chrissie out of the back seat. The aroma of steaks, burgers, or other meat grilling over the fire lingered heavy on the night air from a neighbor's home. Phyllis inhaled the fragrant aroma.

Chrissie moved several steps down the driveway while Phyllis closed the rear car door. "Mommy, Mommy, Mommy!" Chrissie shrieked and pointed a tiny finger toward the front of the house.

"What is it dear?" Phyllis asked glancing around with a curious face. Chrissie pointed a tiny finger at Champion barking and wagging his tail at a cat sleeping under the mosaic planter.

A frown wrinkled her forehead. "Champion, what are you doing outside?" her puzzled voice chided him? Like a greyhound on a racetrack, he made a mad dash toward them, bounding around her legs briskly and wagging his tail from side to side.

"Champy!" Chrissie smiled, showing a gap tooth and giggling as he ran a wet tongue several times up and down her face.

Phyllis eyed her watch. Randy wouldn't be home for another hour. Her thoughts flashed to Wylie. "Come on, you two," Phyllis said.

Champion trotted besides Chrissie. *What's Wylie's excuse tonight?* she wondered. *How could he leave Champion outside unattended? It was really time for him to leave,* she thought as the three of them sauntered to the front door. Near the front door, she eyed an oversized metal lock on the doorknob. The door had been padlocked. Immediately, thoughts flooded her mind about the delinquent mortgage. Time had run out too soon. Couldn't Fidelity of Schenectady have waited a little longer? In a month maybe she could have earned enough in overtime to pay the arrears. Now what? Glancing down, she spotted a twisted piece of paper protruding out of a beer can nestled against the door. She reached down and picked up the empty can that no doubt Wylie had left.

"Sorry, Sis," Wylie's note read. "The sheriff said he had some business to conduct concerning your house. You know I don't hang around for no law. I'm glad what's-his-name will be here to help you later. Your mutt should be all right too. He shot past me like a flash when I opened the door just before the sheriff locked it."

Standing in front of the padlocked door, tears trickled down her face. This couldn't be happening to her! Was she dreaming?

CHAPTER 10

IN LESS THAN a month and a half, the heat would be a thing of the past and fall would announce itself in a splendor of brilliant colors. This afternoon, the mid-August sun settled behind the Adirondack Mountains surrounding the Stockade area, and a hazy glow highlighted the distant peaks.

Phyllis leaned against the padlocked front door of her house. She closed her eyes and exhaled a ragged breath. Looking up at the night sky, a multitude of thoughts swirled in her head concerning the house she no longer owned. Like a bad dream, the situation played on a loop in her mind: Wylie's note, the padlocked door, the foreclosure, and the eviction. This evening's drama preoccupied her thoughts, she didn't keep a watchful eye on Chrissie and Champion playing on the sidewalk.

Her phone chimed several times before she answered the caller. She noticed the time, 9:00 p.m.

"Mom, can I spend the night at Roberto's house? He's cool. His dad is all right too."

"I'd rather you stay home, Randy." She wiped beads of perspiration rising from the brick sidewalk on the second hottest day of the summer. She glanced up at the flock of noisy jaybirds flying around a low branch on a nearby oak tree against a darkening sky. The night shadows soon began to settle around her as the temperature dropped drastically.

"Just for tonight, *please,* Mom. They're having a barbeque later. Mr. McClellan said I'm invited… with your consent."

"How did your community service go this evening?"

"So far, so good. I've completed fifteen hours. Only twenty-five more to go. Mr. Allensworth even told me he might have a job opportunity for me in a couple of weeks. Mom, let me stay tonight *please?*"

Phyllis mused as she held the phone close to her ear. Behind the six-paneled door of her house, their beds awaited them as usual, but tonight it was not possible for Randy to sprint to his bed in his usual manner for a good night's sleep. Was it possible for him to relax in this unfamiliar setting? Her thoughts ran all over the place. The silence answered her.

"I'm not going to get into any trouble, Mom. Just for tonight," Randy pleaded, awaiting his mother's consent on the other end of the cell phone.

Silence hung in the air for a short while longer on her end. Then the thought of Mr. McClellan's kindness stole into her troubled mind. Picking Randy up and dropping him off for community service was a big help. His generosity and thoughtfulness warmed her spirits and brought her into focus again.

"C'mon, Mom!"

Yes, yes. Tonight only," she blurted, coming out of the daze of her thoughts. "Oh, by the way, Chrissie and I are spending the night with Meredith. I'll call you in the morning."

"Cool, looks like we're all hanging out tonight," Randy said in a half chuckle.

"Love you, son. Good night."

"Yeah. Later, Mom."

For a brief moment, her eyes lingered on the oversized metal lock on the wooden door of their Dutch Colonial home. She turned around, scooped Chrissie up with Champion waddling beside her, and shuffled to the car. She buckled Chrissie into her car seat and plopped Champion beside her who was wagging his tail as he did when he was usually taken for a ride. Phyllis scooted into the driver seat, secured her seat belt, then shifted the gear into reverse. It seemed that she just left Meredith's house minutes ago. She'd contact someone to have the padlock removed in the morning. Life would revert to normal…whatever normal was.

Tears pooled in her eyes as she turned the corner to Parker Road, which was lined with Schenectady's historic homes. She thought it seemed like only minutes ago when she rang Meredith's doorbell to pick Chrissie up. She did not want to bother her best friend, but it was getting late. Phyllis yearned to put Chrissie in bed and fluff a pillow under her own drowsy head. When she heard Randy's cell phone click on the other end, her senses returned to reality. Her mind whirled and spun like a Texas tornado. She wrestled with a plethora of thoughts on her way to Meredith's house. She felt like a boxer battered around and cornered by the ropes of anger and frustration in the ring of life. These emotions became her companions. Life's struggles introduced them, now she lived with them daily. Phyllis took in the scenery, occasionally glancing out the window of the sedan. A flood of neon lights passed on either side of the car, and she wondered if the other drivers' problems were worse than hers.

As Chrissie and the cuddly Maltese played on the back seat, she was thankful that neither Randy nor Chrissie felt the full sting of their circumstances yet. Her fear was they eventually would. Their house had just been foreclosed and they were evicted. They had nowhere to call home now. How would Randy react when she told him about the foreclosure and eviction? Would 1789 Mohawk Road become their previous address? Grayson's negligence and irresponsibility as a husband and father in handling the mortgage payments had taken care of that. Now there was nowhere for them to go. Her thoughts immediately flashed to Meredith. She felt certain her best friend would welcome them to stay with open arms until she could find another place. She decided that living with family was out of the question. Wylie was homeless. She had already decided that living with Oscar, Kevin, and other distant and uncaring brothers was not an option as far as she was concerned. Granny Mag lived a couple of hours away in Cooperstown. It wasn't safe for a woman driving alone with kids at night on dark country roads.

After arriving at Meredith's, Champion pawed at the door, whining. Champion's shrill and persistent barking rang in the night air.

Habitually, Meredith would not answer her door at night. Champion was not having it though. He barked and pawed while Phyllis called to Meredith in a desperate tone. Soon the door opened wide.

Meredith's expression said it all. She asked, "Phyllis, what's the matter? I didn't expect to see you so soon." Phyllis' feet were glued in place before she stepped through the threshold. She gave Meredith a blank stare for a brief moment in disbelief of her situation. "I saw you through the peep hole and heard Champion." Meredith stood in the doorway, the lines of her forehead wrinkled in curiosity. "Don't just stand there. Come in, come in." She waved them into the lavish den and reached down to hug Chrissie and rub Champion's fur. "Hello, precious! It's never too soon to see my little princess."

Chrissie's gap-toothed grin beamed wide. Champion nuzzled the furnishing on his first visit in Meredith's home. He gave a jealous bark then leaped onto one of the twin Dutch chairs in the den. The delicious scent of freshly baked cookies still floated on the air. Meredith ambled across the room where Champion made himself at home and gave him a quick nuzzle. Phyllis and Chrissie admired the display of affection.

"What brings you back so soon?"

"Foreclosure. Eviction."

"Gosh! What in the world are you saying, Phyllis?" Unable to hold them back any longer, hot tears spilled down Phyllis's cheeks. Soon the tears became a flowing river as she plopped down on the other twin chair besides Champion. Meredith snatched a tissue box on the end of the coffee table. "Here," she said, handing it to Phyllis. "Come, Chrissie," Meredith said, "let's get you to bed." Phyllis watched as Meredith took Chrissie by the hand and led her out of the den. "Be right back, Phyllis. We'll talk then."

Champion followed behind Meredith into the guest room where Chrissie always stayed on weekends. He waddled beside her into the room like a faithful partner in crime. Meredith quickly dressed Chrissie and put her to bed with Champion cuddling beside her. Meredith ran back into the den and sat beside Phyllis who had moved to the leather sofa.

"Phyllis, what's wrong? Now tell me all about it." Meredith said, dabbing the corner of her own eye.

Phyllis wiped her tears away and spun around to face Meredith. "Nothing, I'm fine."

Meredith's heart sank. With her kindly eyes filled with concern, she moved closer. "We can go into the kitchen. I'll make you some tea." Meredith turned the kettle on and pulled two mugs from the cabinet. Soon the scent of lemony tea drifted into the room.

"I've been a blind failure. If I...I..."

"No ifs, ands, or buts. You are a survivor, Phyllis. Here, drink your tea" Meredith placed the mug in Phyllis' hand who took a few sips. "Nothing happens without God's knowledge, even evil. We learn from bad things, and we grow closer to Him through it all."

Feeling burnt out, Phyllis told Meredith a short version of all her troubles before they both tucked themselves in bed.

The next morning, Phyllis woke up early with the sun filtering through the curtain. Squinting her eyes against the sunlight beneath the window shade, she stretched in the downy bed like a contented cat and enjoyed the stillness for a few minutes. She mentally sketched out an agenda for the day. More than ever, she was determined to settle things in her family's life and restore life back to normal again. She strode to the room where Chrissie slept and watched her chest rise and fall in tender sleep. Last night had been hard on her too. Champion resembled a fluffy cotton ball snoozing in his dog-tired way next to Chrissie. Phyllis smiled as she folded her arms across her chest. She tiptoed out so that she would not disturb anyone and strode to the bathroom to shower and get dressed for the day.

Ready to accomplish her plan to get access into the house, she felt more exuberant. She hastily dressed in a red short-sleeved top. The price tag was still dangling off it as well as the stonewashed jeans that Meredith had given her on last night with the pj's. Thank goodness they both wore a size ten.

Chrissie already had lots of clothes, sundresses, and other outfits in the closet for her weekend visits at Meredith's. They hung on child-size hangers. Some were still wrapped in their original packaging that Meredith recently bought. She often shopped for Chrissie.

She couldn't have children so Chrissie, in many ways, became her own daughter.

In the kitchen, the coffee's invigorating aroma filled the entire home.

"Hi!" Meredith was already sipping a cup of black coffee in the kitchen nook. Phyllis sent her a cheery greeting, heading to the round glass table with more pep in her stride than she had on last night. The large bay window in the breakfast nook accentuated the cozy area. "Glad to see you're in better spirits," said Meredith. "Dig in. It's one of your favorites, sausage and bacon casserole."

"How can I ever thank you? You're a gem!" Summer fruit was served on a crystal bowl in the middle of the table. "Freshly squeezed orange juice and homemade cinnamon buns too!" Phyllis was pouring herself a cup of juice. Phyllis chomped on the scrumptious meal in a hurry. "Meredith I have to get access to the house. I'm driving over there after breakfast."

"But, Phyll, the door is padlocked."

"I have a plan. I hope it doesn't fail. Hope *I* don't fail," Phyllis exclaimed, exhaling a large breath.

"You must not even consider failure. You're stronger than you realize. Let me help. I can drop Chrissie off at Lil Tots. That'll save some time. Deal?" Meredith asked, brown eyes staring at Phyllis who was tilting her head to the side. Several locks of corkscrew curls fell over her shoulder.

"Deal!" Phyllis said with a warm smile.

Ten minutes later, Phyllis pulled into the familiar driveway toward the garage. She called Rylander earlier who agreed to give her the day off. Mentally, she checked that task off her laundry list of things to do. Seconds after Phyllis got out of the sedan, a familiar voice distracted her.

"Good morning, Phyllis." Claire Nugent, her neighbor, was hiking in her direction with King, their Boston terrier trotting beside her. They usually go to the park for their daily morning walk.

"I saw the van from Metro Movers in front of your house about an hour ago. She craned her neck toward the front of the house. "You're leaving our neighborhood? We'll miss you."

"Why, no…no," Phyllis stammered. She walked past the mosaic lily and sped up the sidewalk to the front door, leaving Claire gaping. She planned to use the remote to the garage and enter through the den. The movers surely would have a key to the padlock.

Two men dressed in faded green uniforms labeled Metro Movers had already placed the "Foreclosure" sign in the yard. They were pushing the chrome double-door fridge strapped to a dolly over the threshold. A younger, lanky man wearing a cap backward nearly stumbled. The bushy-eyed older man steadied the dolly. Phyllis raced past them through the doorway like a zap of lighting.

"Whoa! Ma'am, not so fast," said Chuck, the older man whose thick brows protruded like a broom over his eyes. The short stocky man was resting the fridge down on the sidewalk on the dolly. A cigarette dangled out of one side of his mouth. His coworker, Ricky, the lanky one, threw his hands up.

Phyllis froze near the entrance of the house. "This is my house," she assured them.

"Not anymore. We got orders to move everything. Foreclosure, ma'am."

"Please, I must get some clothes. I have children. I have important documents."

"Sorry. We don't make the rules and can't let you break them."

"Please," she pleaded, her voice trembling. "I must get some of my things." She ran a palm below her eyes to wipe the sweat on her face while she talked.

"Ma'am, I'm not s'pose to let you in here. It's against company policy. Guess won't hurt none to let you take your important things. Ma'am, hurry up. My boss don't take kindly to us disobeying orders."

"Never could stand a bawling woman," said Chuck to his coworker. "Go ahead…but hurry. If anybody says anything, we don't know *nuthin'*, ya hear?"

Phyllis nodded and ran straight to her bedroom. She grabbed the keys out of a chest, unlocked the file cabinet, and snatched the folder out labeled "important documents" and set it on the dresser. Quickly she grabbed an armful of her favorite suits and ran downstairs. She piled the outfits on the sofa to be placed in the car later.

In a mad dash, she rushed upstairs to Randy's room where she picked up an armful of his clothes scattered on the floor and grabbed his laptop before going back to her room to get Randy's MP3 player and other devices. Loaded down, she raced to the car and gently deposited the electronic gadgets on the floor in the back of the car and covered them with some of the clothes to hide them. Realizing the movers could boot her out any minute, she worked fast. She clutched Chrissie's favorite dolls under her arm. A pearl necklace dangled out of the jewelry box. Phyllis crumpled on the side of the bed and reflected on the wedding gift her Mom had given her on her wedding day. Memories of her mother giving her up on her sixth birthday crashed in on her. Suzette was a strong woman. Phyllis recalled that her dad passed away when she was four. Her mom struggled to raise five kids, especially with Oscar and Wylie constantly in trouble. Her mom had explained that Granny Mag would take good care of her only daughter.

"Hey, lady! You gotta get out of here. Can't stay much longer."

The voice jerked Phyllis back to reality. "I'm almost done!" she hollered back.

Striding through the doorway with a pearl necklace dangling in her hand and several photos, she sprinted down the sidewalk. Her gaze shifted to the edge of the curb and spotted the headlines of the *Daily Gazette* in bold letters, "Move-in special and one month rent-free for Hampshire Apartments." She reached down, grabbed the newspaper from the sidewalk, coiled it into a cylinder under her arms, and hiked to the car. The headlines piqued her interest, and she planned to check it out. The short distance to the car seemed longer as her thoughts turned into questions. How could she part with her house, her fine furniture, and her life? She glanced at the headlines and a faint grin etched her face. A gleam of hope spread across her dimpled cheeks.

CHAPTER 11

PHYLLIS SAT IN the car that was still parked in the driveway, recovering from the hard work of packing and loading the family's belongings. Sitting behind the steering wheel, she concentrated on her next plan of action. Immediately, her thoughts drifted to Randy. A crease furrowed her forehead. Was he okay? She pulled her cell phone from her purse in the glove compartment. She tapped the speed button with a finger, dialing Randy's cell number.

"Hello, Mom?"

"How are you, son? Are you okay?" she asked, playing with a loose curl from her frazzled ponytail.

"Yeah, I'm good."

"I'm afraid I have some bad news. We've lost our house in a foreclosure."

"Foreclosure! Mom, how could you let that happen?" The irritation in Randy's voice normally wouldn't faze Phyllis. This time, she thought his reaction was understandable. Her initial reaction to the travesty had been the same. How could Randy have known that his dad had been the culprit? How could he have known that Grayson had been negligent in paying the mortgage and the other bills? "Can I stay with Roberto? His dad said I could stay till the weekend. We're looking for evening jobs."

"Fine, but have Mr. McClelland call me. I want you home for the weekend. We'll have another place by then." Phyllis glanced at the time on her watch and could not believe it was a quarter past noon already. Time passed with a dizzying tempo. She worked feverishly to load the car with as many of their belongings as it would hold. The angry growl in her stomach attested to her hunger pains. She started the engine and shifted the gear into reverse before steering the car up North Church Street. Restaurants dotted the streets on either side of the blocks. Sometime later, Phyllis turned the corner onto Grover Avenue and parked in front of one of Schenectady's favorite hang-outs. El Divino Steak and Ale was reasonably priced, the reason for its popularity in town. It was a good choice since she decided to be modest with her spending until her finances improved.

"Howdy, ma'am!" a stocky man said in a deep voice. Clad in a wide-brimmed white hat with the edges turned up, he stood in the doorway like Matt Dillon facing a gunslinger at high noon. A brown leather buckle sat around his thick waist that matched his pointed-toe boots.

Phyllis gave him a faint smile and waited for him to exit the doorway to prevent squeezing past him. He moved the toothpick in his mouth from side to side and folded broad arms across his chest while gazing down at her in a manner too friendly. "Good day, sir," Phyllis said, trying to move past him.

Realizing her lack of interest, he said, "Good day, ma'am." He tipped his broad hat and winked at her.

She nodded and walked past him into the lounge area of the touristy restaurant. The aroma of grilled burgers and steaks greeted her while servers scurried across the room, hefting large platters over their heads and delivering savory orders. Sparks from the grill flew into the air as the sizzling sound of burgers and steaks made a sym-phony of sound. The red-and-blue-checkered tablecloths in the large room give it a Southern country feel.

A familiar chuckle rang across the room from a corner table. "Hello, Phyll." Zel's bony finger beckoned Phyllis to their table that was off the doorway. Georgette's head rocked back and forth in lighthearted laughter. She was one of their giddy classmates, Phyllis remembered. Phyllis strode to the table, pulled out a chair, and sat down wearily. A waitress took her order. "Good timing. We're final-izing the plans for our class reunion in a couple of weeks," Zel said.

"Let's celebrate the good ole days and the great memories of Lincoln High. Okay, girls?"

"Right," Georgette and Lydia responded with a nod of their heads.

"You promised to help us when we asked you to join us at the Walkabout Faire," Georgette reminded Phyllis.

"Gee, I'm sorry. I won't be able to help or stay long, especially today. I planned to grab a quick lunch and then keep an urgent appointment I have on the north side of town."

"Come on, Phyll," they echoed in unison. Georgette skewed her face into a pouting smirk.

"All right." A smile widened across her face as she shifted her gazed from each classmate to the other. "But only for a little while. Deal?"

"Okay, it's a deal, but you owe us one," Lydia said in her squeaky voice.

A luscious aroma filled Phyllis's nostrils as the waiter plopped the steak burger platter laden with golden fries on the table in front of her. "Excuse me, what would you like to drink?" The waiter interrupted their conversation to ask for Phyllis' response.

"Water with a slice of lemon please." She scooped the famous oversized burger from the platter and nibbled a small bite of it. She hoped to have good news for Meredith this evening. Hanging out with classmates was not on her agenda today. No time for lollygagging, she had to hurry to the Hampshire apartment soon.

Keeping in character with her obvious nosiness, Georgette sat at the corner of the table facing the doorway where she had more than a bird's-eye view and was within an earshot of people entering the restaurant. The conversation was too engaged that Georgette missed the fiasco with her and the cowboy when Phyllis entered the restaurant. "Well, look who's here!" Georgette suddenly blurted, rising from her seat. She beckoned for Brett Moreland, one of their high school classmates, to join them. They were unaware of his recent relocation to Schenectady.

"How do I deserve the pleasure of five beautiful ladies brightening up my world?" he asked, staring directly into Phyllis's eye. Phyllis remained unengaged as she kept munching on the oversized burger. She dabbed on the corner of her mouth with a napkin. A bright smile lit Brett's lean chiseled face. He gleamed a handsome smile as he enveloped each woman in a fleeting hug before joining them.

"Don't you look debonair," said Georgette as she ran her fingers over the satiny sleeve of Brett's suit jacket.

Even during high school, Brett typically wore designer suits. Although he was fastidious about his appearance, his family's wealth did not spoil him. Brett displayed the perfect model of unpretentious humility. Today, he sported a gray suit with a matching silk tie. He pulled off the jacket and carefully lapped it over the back of the chair. Brett pulled up a chair and sat across the table from Zel who was adjacent to Lydia. He sent Phyllis a private look, his eyes lingering on her for a brief while. Phyllis' gaze caught his. Something seemed to pass between them. Awareness? Concern? Surprise? Before she could decide, Zel spoke and interrupted his thoughts.

Out of the corner of her eye, Zel noticed the spark in Brett's eye. She reached her arm across the table to touch his. "Earth to Brett," she said, giving his shirt a gentle yank to bring him back into reality.

"Hungry?" Lydia asked Brett.

"Yes." He was actually starving. "Anything good on the menu today?" he asked Lydia.

A spirited young waiter scampered to their table and handed Brett a menu. After placing his order, the energetic waiter took his order and soon brought a large pecan-crusted chicken salad and a tall glass of lemonade to help wash it down.

Zel's curiosity got the best of her. "The class reunion is a couple weeks away. What brings you to town so soon?"

Georgette placed a palm on either side of her face with both elbows on the table and leaned closer with searching eyes. Phyllis settled back in her seat, seemingly unnoticed by the girls.

"Thank God I finally passed the medical board. I'm here for an interview with the Children's Hospital."

"Congratulations, *Dr.* Brett Moreland!" they said sarcastically.

He gave them an Elvis Presley impression, "Thank you very much!"

Phyllis finished eating and grabbed the bill the waiter placed beside her platter. "Brett, it was nice seeing you again. Girls, I gotta go." She rose to leave.

"Phyll, you owe us one!" they shouted in unison.

"I gotta go as well," Brett said. He sipped the last of the lemonade and jumped up as Phyllis was leaving. "It's been really great. I'll see all of you at the reunion."

"Hope all goes well with your interview," Zel said, looking up at Brett. Lydia and Georgette smiled and waved a friendly goodbye. "Let's get back to business," Zel resumed. "Anyone know of a good local DJ?" she asked Georgette and Lydia.

Brett nabbed the bill from the table and jogged to the counter to catch up with Phyllis who quickly paid her bill and was about to exit the restaurant. He caught up with her outside before she got in the car. "Phyllis, I hope to see you at our upcoming reunion," he said, facing her.

Phyllis drew in a lengthy breath. "Sure," she said as she pulled her purse over her shoulders. She realized she was curt and she did not mean to be mean, but seeing Brett today triggered an uneasy feeling that she wasn't ready to deal with at the time. Phyllis noticed the questioning look on his face. She could not deal with any distraction from her top priority of taking care of her family. The *Daily Gazette* headlines that announced the move-in special at the Hampshire Apartments played over in her mind as she drove to the north side of Schenectady. She hoped that the advertisement for one month's free rent was still current.

Brett's face swam back in her mind. His firm jaw and those dark brown eyes melted her heart when they dated in high school and for a little while in college. He was just a kid then who promised to make her dreams come true. His smile also played over in her mind. This was so unlike her to reflect on a man who may be a happily married man. She pulled her thoughts together and focused on her agenda.

The drive to the Hampshire Apartments gave her time to think and plan. Upon arrival, Phyllis took in the natural beauty of the area. Colorful hydrangeas, tulips, and snapdragons scented the air surrounding the elegant apartment. Pine branches waved their long arms in the late August heat and seem to welcome Phyllis to the place she hoped would be her new home. She quickened her steps as she paced down the well-groomed sidewalk. A bright smile spread across her face as she reached the door labeled "Rental Office." Taking care of Randy and Chrissie topped Phyllis's priority list. Meredith's kindness was appreciated, but today she prayed to leave with a place of her own.

"How may I help you?" the receptionist asked Phyllis as she entered the elegant rental office.

"I'd like to make an application for a two- or maybe three-bedroom apartment."

"Great, please be seated. I'll get the manager for you. His name is Mr. Pennington. He can qualify you today."

"Would you like to see our spacious floor plans first?"

"Yes, thank you," Phyllis answered with a smile.

"Right this way please." The buxom brunette showed Phyllis several floor plans for the two and three bedrooms with each price quote. Phyllis completed the lengthy credit application and gave it to the receptionist. "You're welcome to the coffee and tea while you wait in the sitting area," the receptionist said.

Phyllis thanked her and made herself comfortable in the plush Queen Anne chair and sipped on a diet soda while waiting for the application to be approved.

"Hello, Ms. Whitmore. I'm Mr. Pennington, the manager, and I'll run your application." After fifteen minutes, Mr. Pennington gave Phyllis the results. "I'm sorry but your application has been denied."

"Denied?" Phyllis asked surprisingly setting her cup on the receptionist's desk. "Why?"

"I'm sorry. It appears you don't have enough credit established in your name." Do you know someone who can cosign your application?"

"No."

"I know where you can maybe receive approval more easily. A new development has been recently built near Hamilton Hill. They're always looking for new residents." He scribbled the address on a piece of paper and gave it to Phyllis who thanked him, stared at the address for a moment, and then left.

There was no time to weigh every option. Did she really have another option? She was settled on the fact that she'd get a place of her own and get her family's lives back on track. After Phyllis got back into her car, she sensed a tinge of trepidation but kept her hopes high. Her lips muttered a silent prayer as she sped to the address that the manager had given her.

Ridgeway Courts introduced itself as a newly built housing complex in various ways. The Courts, as it was called, recently celebrated its fifth birthday. More than a few vacant lots were scattered between some of the already cramped houses. Some lots only had the foundation poured with no other signs of building the home. The Courts stretched itself out between the older and well-established Hamilton Hill area. Phyllis thought it seemed like a planet away from the Stockade. Her gaze scanned the surrounding area. Graffiti marred several buildings. Aging McDonald's cups and hamburger wrappers lay fading along the street curbs and empty beer cans littered the sidewalk. The nicely built brick homes stood a little more than arm's length between each house. Phyllis drove past the main entrance and turned to Misty Heights Lane toward the rental office. Her spirits dropped. She couldn't decide if she wanted to turn around or not. She lived in the Stockade most of her life. Its opulence was not the same here.

CHAPTER 12

BRETT'S GAZE SHOT upward in gratitude as he exited the double glass doors of the Children's Hospital of Schenectady. He came down the hospital steps with strides that would easily compete with the penguin's dance steps in the movie *Happy Feet*. Brett left Dr. Eric Jolik's office, the head of pediatrics, on a high note. A month ago, he had interviewed via a brief conference call. Today he aced the face-to-face interview. In a couple of weeks, he'd start work as Dr. Jolik's assistant. The realization washed over him, and he relished the idea.

His mind jerked back to seeing Phyllis today at the restaurant. The memory drew him back to their high school years when they first met. The thought of her made him smile. He recalled the day he asked her to marry him. He promised to make all of her dreams come true that day. Since high school, time, circumstances and distance separated them. He wanted to rekindle the passion but the timing wasn't right yet. He couldn't allow those feelings to surface to their fullest today.

Still Brett couldn't get Phyllis out of his mind. He felt like a high school kid all over again. Phyllis' reaction today seemed nonchalant and indifferent to him. He sensed that she was preoccupied. Maybe she was married? No, he didn't notice the glint of a diamond on her finger. He'd see her at the class reunion in a few weeks and try to reestablish their relationship.

* * *

Grayson Whitmore sat alone in his furnished condo. Both hands cupped his face where he sat on an unmade bed with his head lowered and eyes staring at the thickly carpeted floor. A frown etched his face as he ran his hands through dark wavy hair. Rising from the bed, he strolled to the window of the spacious room decorated in hues of red and gold. Fine furniture spelled lavishness in every corner. He slid the curtain to the side and looked down from one vehicle to another, speeding along to various destinations. "Scurrying to work," he reckoned. He should be in his Mercedes driving to work himself. That was his life until a week ago when he received a phone call from the corporate office.

"Bruner and Bruner, Grayson speaking," he answered the phone.

On the other end, the caller from corporate expounded on the details that Bruner and Bruner was downsizing immediately. Grayson remembered the silence that lingered on his end for a long while before the conversation continued. "We're sorry we have to let you and the other employees go. Engineering services are being contracted out to Westgate and Fields, Inc. You'll still have a job, just another position."

The phone call regarding the company downsizing ruined his day, ruined his marriage to Phyllis, and ruined his relationship with Randy and Chrissie. How could he face them as a loser? The CEO status made Grayson feel important, a feeling he longed to receive from his dad but had never gotten. Since he'd lost his position of Bruner and Bruner Engineering Corporation his six-figure salary dwindled significantly. His thoughts were all over the place. Hard work and extra-long hours had taken a toll on him, although he'd spent a weekend vacation on the island of Aruba after the divorce that now seemed like years ago.

"I should be sitting at my desk as the CEO," he muttered out loud. "I should be with Phyllis and the kids." He sang his sad song to himself. A silk blue necktie lay crumpled across the foot of the bed. The matching jacket kept it company there with two days of dirty socks. The spacious room scented the air with cologne, not alcohol. Grayson vowed to never be an alcoholic like his dad, so he became a workaholic. A myriad of thoughts ran through his mind concerning the things he needed to change. He needed to start with child support payments. He missed Randy and Chrissie. Maybe he'd look into that today, but he couldn't face Phyllis. He didn't want her to look on the loser that he'd become. He called her at home but received no answer. Apparently, she blocked his number on her cell phone. Could he blame her? Meredith could help him contact her, he thought. He'd feel redeemed for that much.

* * *

"May I see your vacancies for a two- or three-bedroom apartment please? Phyllis asked the white-bearded heavyset man when she entered the leasing office.

"We just rented the last two-bedroom apartment last week," he responded in an apologetic manner. "But we have several one-bedroom units left. Would you be interested in seeing them?"

"No, I really need at least two bedrooms," she said.

"Let's see," he said, sitting down behind the desk. He pulled up the screen on the computer with the list of available apartments. "Three one-bedrooms," he muttered under his breath while studying the screen. "Well, what do you know, a cancellation for apartment 13F." Phyllis stood at his desk, waiting with high hopes. In the background, she heard music from a gospel station played inspirational tunes. "I guess you're in luck. We have one three-bedroom available but it won't be ready till Saturday morning. Just need to spruce it up with a fresh coat of paint. It's one of our furnished apartments. It'll cost you more," he said with emphasis.

"Saturday morning is fine," Phyllis answered, beaming. She extended a handshake to the gentleman, hoping that the extra cost would fit her budget.

"Ma'am, I'll need to take your application first." He handed her a short form to fill out.

This time, Phyllis completed the application only in her name. In a short while, she returned the completed application to the rental agent. The silver-haired man keyed the information into the computer. In a few minutes, the status came back "Approved."

"How much more for the apartment?"

"Our fully furnished apartment run an extra one hundred-twenty-five dollars per month." Phyllis nodded in agreement and whispered a prayer at the same time. She ran out of options. She'd take it and trust the man upstairs that she could afford the payments. "Apartment 13F is around the corner on the end. Ready to go see it?" he asked, his brown eyes sparkling.

In a few minutes, he opened the lock on the apartment. Phyllis moved ahead of the agent and entered the cramped layout of the living room. Her eyes widened and flickered in surprise but mostly gratitude. The room was small but neat and clean. A brown faux leather sofa and matching love seat kept each other company along the eggshell-colored wall with white trim. She walked into the kitchen and gazed at the bright cozy room with a hint of yellow walls lined with several cabinets. A short Formica counter and a small maple table surrounded by four chairs sat in the middle of the room. An arch opened on the left to a narrow hallway with a bathroom in between. Blinds hung over a single double-paned window that looked out on the noisy street from the kitchen's view.

"Like it?" he asked.

"I love it!" she said, stepping further into the furnished room. *Why not?* she thought. *Lavish? No, but it was hers.*

"Well, I'm glad you like it, ma'am."

This was a place for her, Randy, and Chrissie. It was her dream coming true. Under her breath, she whispered thanks in her heart to the Man upstairs. Although the area left much to be desired, which was a concern for her, at least the apartment was decent. She'd make do. "Thank you, Mr. Molinger."

Later that evening, Phyllis pulled into Meredith's driveway and dashed into the house.

"What's that look all about?" Meredith asked. She cocked her head to the side, searching at Phyllis' expression. Her eyes lingered on the sparkle in her friend's dark brown eyes.

"I've rented an apartment, and it's in my own name," she said, placing a hand on her hip. I'm moving on Saturday morning."

Her dimples deepened. The joy and exhilaration in her voice was contagious.

"Saturday? That's wonderful!" Meredith wrapped her arms around Phyllis with all her might. "Praise God! He never lets His children down. Come on, let's celebrate. The last batch of chocolate chip cookies are in the oven."

With a wide grin that matched Phyllis', Meredith's curls bounced over her face as she and her best friend scurried to the kitchen like two kids eager for a snack.

* * *

Randy opened the door of the Lexus and climbed in it on Saturday morning. Phyllis picked him up before 8:00 a.m. Randy's appetite demanded that they grab a quick breakfast from McDonald's before going to the apartment.

Meredith followed Phyllis in her green pickup truck. Chrissie, buckled in the back seat, played with the Barbie doll that Meredith bought her earlier in the week. Champion snuggled close to Chrissie. Cleaning supplies and the belongings that Phyllis managed to bring from the foreclosed house lay neatly stashed in the corner of the truck. Several weeks ago, the late August sun blazed like an inferno. This morning, the chilly wind stirred briskly across Schenectady. September announced fall with its threat of cooler weather to follow in the upcoming weeks. Meredith followed behind Phyllis into Ridgeway Courts. Driving past her, she turned to Carol Wills Drive and parked in front of Apartment 13F. She, Chrissie, and Champion waited in the car for Phyllis to return with the keys.

Phyllis got out of the car and bounded to the door. She turned the key with pride. "Come in and see the apartment. Meredith, I'm sure you've noticed that this place is no match for the stockade mansions. It's suitable though until child support starts. Maybe we can get a bigger place soon." Even now when she pictured Grayson, her stomach churned. He promised to make her dreams come true. *Would Brett have ever let her down?* she wondered.

Meredith entered the apartment and glanced around. "It's homey." She tried to see the small home as Phyllis saw it. It didn't look so bad, small but well-maintained. Phyllis had a place of her own for her and the kids. For that, she was grateful.

Chrissie and Champion walked from room to room, exploring the apartment. A smile lit Phyllis' face. She noticed Meredith brown eyes light up as she watched Chrissie and Champion roam the place. Randy retrieved his clothes and other things that were packed in her car. When he entered the living room, she noticed his frown. He brushed past her and Meredith as they stood near the sofa. Randy went back to the bedroom like an unhappy camper. Earlier he was arguing with Kerry Mitterson. Phyllis hoped his girlfriend was the cause of his frustration, not their new home.

Hours later, Meredith and Phyllis finished cleaning, dusting, and freshening up of the apartment.

"Time for lunch," Meredith said, smiling.

"Sounds good to me," Phyllis said, anticipating the delicacies.

Meredith set a plate of barbecue sandwiches warmed in the microwave on the Formica counter. She bought the sandwiches earlier this morning from a nearby deli. The aroma of barbecue filled the room when she set the piping hot sandwiches on the kitchen table. Phyllis watched Meredith's brown eyes sparkled with exhilaration as she worked. She uncovered and arranged a relish tray, dump a pile of Lay's potato chips in a large bowl, and a set a small tray of chocolate chip cookies next to the sandwiches. Cans of soft drinks were also set on the table.

"Come on guys, let's eat! Meredith announced stepping in the hallway to project her voice loud enough for Randy to hear.

Randy hurried to the table, cell phone glued to his ears, bickering with Kerry Mitterson. They had been arguing for hours, it seemed. He grabbed four large sandwiches, extra helping of chips, a soda, and raced to his room to continue arguing with Kerry.

"What's that noise?" Phyllis asked.

"I hear it too, said Meredith.

Together they rushed to the living room window and peered out of it in the direction of the noise. A dog and a cat were fighting in the street. "Scram, you ugly monsters!"

Phyllis heard her neighbor in apartment 13G holler at a stray dog and his scraggly companion. Clydie Newsome showed a row of tobacco-stained teeth with more than a few teeth missing at the bottom. Strands of gray hair pulled back tightly in a bun on her four-foot frame that weighed more than a half side of beef.

Phyllis and Meredith watched as she exited her apartment door-way with three overweight cats waddling behind her. Two kittens stumbled at her heels. They plodded down the sidewalk. A stray German shepherd and his companion followed, barking their objections to Clydie's feline companions. The cats hissed and howled at the barking dogs. Phyllis gave Meredith a blank stare. Meredith's eyes lingered on Phyllis. She was afraid of cats.

"Cats!" Phyllis said in disgust. She heaved her chest and exhaled an exasperated breath. "Come on, Meredith. We have a celebration to get back."

They left the living room and strutted back to the kitchen.

CHAPTER 13

PHYLLIS STOLE OUT of bed early Sunday morning. After overnight showers, cooler temps had set in and chilled the air. She quickly dressed in a white fleece robe and darted to the kitchen to make a pot of coffee. Sitting at the kitchen table, Phyllis savored the warmth of a cup of Folgers dark roast. The coffee's invigorating and fragrant aroma filled the small quaint kitchen.

"Kerry, that's it! I'm done!" She overheard Randy's stern voice roar from his bedroom.

Yelling at his girlfriend, Phyllis thought, *he'll be hungry after that argument.* She walked to the apartment-size fridge and removed a carton of milk and orange juice. Then she took two bowls from the cabinet above the fridge and a family-size cereal box from the cupboards. She set the square oak table with the milk, cereal, and a pitcher of juice for a light breakfast. Phyllis decided to check on her little tot and the Maltese. Chrissie and Champion, both lightly snoring, were snuggled together in bed. Phyllis leaned against the doorway and folded her arms across her chest. A broad grin covered her face. "Sheer exhaustion," she muttered under her breath, smiling and shaking her head side to side. She went back into the kitchen to finish her cup of coffee and bowl of cereal. Phyllis enjoyed the quiet, peaceful moment. A good cup of hot coffee and the comfort of being settled in her own place.

"It's over Kerry!" Randy hollered into his cell phone as he entered the kitchen.

Phyllis noticed that the anger in his voice matched the scowl covering his face. She was elated he just ended his relationship with Kerry. She wished it had been sooner. Throwing his hands into the air, Randy plopped down on a chair at the kitchen table. "How did you sleep last night?" Phyllis asked.

"Sleep? How could I? That old windbag and those cats would wake the dead in a morgue." He extended his long arms and grabbed the frosted cornflakes, poured a bowl, and doused them with milk.

"How many hours do you need to complete your community service? Have you been attending your meetings regularly?" Phyllis asked.

"Questions, questions, more questions. Gimme a break, Mom. Just two more weeks of community service and I'm done."

"Watch your mouth young man!" Phyllis retorted.

She took another sip of the steaming coffee and quickly left the table. Phyllis carried her bowl to the sink and rinsed it. She lifted her head up as if staring at the ceiling. *Lord, let your hand become my help*, she whispered in her heart. She tried to tell herself that her life would soon get better, that Randy would change. He had been unhappy with everything she did. Today was no exception. Despite all of Phyllis' triumphs, in Randy's eyes, she was a total failure. The divorce, house foreclosure, and now a cramped dinky apartment with an old windbag and cats for a neighbor. Phyllis managed to get his iPod, iPad, MP3 player, and even his favorite chess game from their foreclosed home, but he still didn't appreciate her efforts. Randy finished his cereal and jumped up from the table. He brushed past his mom and stormed out of the apartment. Phyllis watched him bolt through the door in a burst of his typical anger.

The sun came out after last night's showers, so did the kids at Ridgeway Court.

Randy headed in the opposite direction of the apartment. He walked a short distance when he heard shouts of excitement wailing through the air. He noticed four guys glistening with sweat as they slammed hoops on the basketball court next to the recreation center a few feet away. Still stewing, Randy kicked a crumpled Coca-Cola can down the street. He kept his head lowered as he walked toward the Center. A crowd of kids had gathered around the center, laughing and hanging out. Looking around, he sized up the area. *The center seemed to be the headquarters for fun at Ridgeway Courts*, he thought. He lowered his head and continued kicking the crushed can.

"Hey, you! What are you doing in this neighborhood?" hollered Lance Collier, approaching Randy from a short distance.

Randy stopped in his tracks. A few feet from him, a towering, muscular blond was calling him out. He appeared to be a few inches taller than him and maybe a year older. He'd seen bullies at school and avoided them. His pulse quickened, fear pumping through his veins. He started walking again toward the recreational center as if he didn't hear him. He was no pushover, but Lance looked intimidating. Lance was one of Ridgeway Courts worst neighborhood buillies. With short dirty blond hair over his rounded face, he shoved Randy to the ground.

"Leave him alone!" a firm voice called out nearby.

Randy spotted three teenage boys running from the basketball court toward him. Lance spun around and bolted in the opposite direction like a ravenous lion chasing after its prey. Sprawled on the pavement, Randy groaned in an effort to scramble to his feet.

Jody, Pierce, and Emilio raced to the scene. They had been watching Randy walking toward the center from the court. Jody turned his sparsely pimpled face toward Pierce, winked an eye, and elbowed him. Lance had taken off like a bolt of lightning. He had a run-in with Jody before and lost.

"A go do it," Pierce immediately responded in his Guyanese dialect.

He understood what his leader meant and leaned his stubby body down, exposing a scar on his right cheek. He grabbed Randy's hands and pulled him to his feet. Emilio's dark golden skin shone in the sunlight, his Mohawk haircut accentuated his round face.

Heat and pain seared Randy's flesh as he tried to balance himself. "Thanks," he said, grateful for the timely help.

"Don't worry about Lance Collier," said Jody. "He won't bother you anymore. He's trouble around here, but he gives us *our* respect." Jody gave Pierce and Emilio each a fist bump.

"Cool," said Randy. A grin pulled at the corner of his mouth.

"This is Emilio, and that's Pierce. I'm Jody. You new in the neighborhood?"

"Yeah," Randy nodded, shifting his gaze from one boy to the other as he studied them for a moment.

Jody placed a friendly slap on Randy's back, garnering a chuckle from Pierce and Emilio. "Up for a game of pool?" Pierce asked.

A grin crossed Randy's face. They went to play a lengthy game of pool then ping-pong. Tonguing a toothpick.

"Would you like to join our gang?" asked Jody, leaning against the side of the pool table with legs crossed at the ankle.

His new friends rescued him. Randy thought it would be great to belong to a gang, one that wasn't so bad. He heard how bad gangs could be, but these guys seemed pretty cool.

Jody filled Randy in on the Hillside Dominators and their expectation of him, more like what's not expected of him. "Meet us tomorrow night at the old Nottingham building around eight thirty."

They watched Randy leave them on an emotional high.

* * *

The autumn chill carried over into Monday morning. Phyllis left her apartment earlier to accommodate the longer drive to Chrissie's day care and Randy's school. On her way to Lil Tots after work, Phyllis mused as she drove. Zel called earlier that morning about the class reunion next Saturday. The event would be held at the Omni, Schenectady's new five-star hotel. "Two nights of fun and excitement," Zel had said.

"America the Beautiful" chimed on her cell phone. "He did what?" Phyllis exclaimed in a loud burst of anger.

"He called me," answered Meredith. "After you left, he called me late Saturday night."

"Grayson is a chicken," Phyllis told Meredith. "He should have called me himself. Instead, he's bothering you with his troubles."

Meredith let out a long sigh. "He can't face you, Phyllis. But I do have some good news."

"No news would be good news about Grayson. He's the bad news," Phyllis said in an unforgiving voice.

"He tried to call you but couldn't get a hold of you. Grayson says he's ready to pay child support," said Meredith in an elated voice.

"It's about time!" Quickly calming herself, she added, "I guess I did block his number. So much for that. Sorry Meredith," Phyllis said apologetically. "Changing the subject, Zel called about our upcoming class reunion next Saturday. I need a favor. Can I borrow a dress?"

"How about we go shopping, Phyll? I'd love for us both to get something new."

"I'm on a tight budget."

"No problem, I got this one," said Meredith cheerfully. "Is Saturday morning good for our shopping spree?"

"Saturday sounds great," Phyllis graciously agreed.

Phyllis arrived at the day care minutes later. At the parking lot, she called Randy who was already on the bus heading home when he answered. "Mom, I have a community service meeting tonight at six. Mr. McClelland offered to pick me up with Roberto. Roberto completed his community service two weeks ago, but likes the girls—uh, his group project and still wants me to come. Mr. Allensworth said it was okay."

"Sounds good," said Phyllis, "but I'll call Mr. McClelland."

* * *

"All right. I need everyone to listen up," said Mr. Allensworth. "I need group number three to go to the rotunda now. Group number two, I'll need you to stay here. Mrs. Allensworth is putting the finishing touches on some stuff for you to work on. She'll come in shortly."

Mr. Allensworth exited the room and led group three down the long hallway to the rotunda. Randy filed out of the room with Toby McPhie, Bobbie Hilrodden, and the other kids assigned to his group. "Our church is sending relief to the tornado victims in Scottsdale. We have to package these boxes," he said at the rotunda. "Let's form teams of two. After you've packed all the boxes, meet back in the area where group two is assembled."

Sarah Rose and Melanie strolled into the room as Mr. Allensworth completed his directions. Randy eyed Sarah Rose and hiked to where she and Melanie stood.

"Mr. McClelland said to form teams of two. Want to team up with me?" Randy asked Sarah Rose.

"Sure." Her hazel eyes beamed like an angel.

She waved Melanie good-bye and watched her saunter to the table in the back with Toby McPhie. She turned to see Randy's eyes fixed on her. A sheepish look etched her face as she lowered her gaze and reached for a blanket to place inside the box.

"Oh, we'd better start packing these boxes," said Randy. He felt a familiar sensation in his stomach that he felt when he first saw her. Butterflies flitted in his stomach. Randy and Sarah Rose chattered back and forth like two elementary kids on a playground.

All the youth assembled again in the meeting room.

"Quick announcement," said Mr. Allensworth with a booming voice. "Our church carnival is Saturday morning at ten. You're all invited, and you can bring a friend. Questions anyone?" Silence. "That's great." He said a prayer over the group and dismissed them.

"Sarah Rose, can I call you?" Randy asked, referring to her by her full name.

"Sure," she said and gave him her cell number, which he immediately saved in his phone.

Randy dashed out of the room with a broad smile to find Roberto. After the meeting, Roberto's dad drove Randy straight home. Randy checked the time on his cell phone, 8:15 p.m. He promised to meet Jody, Pierce, and Emilio at 8:30 at the old Nottingham building. He'd have to hurry. His mom would not miss him. She thinks that he and Roberto were still attending their community service meeting. The old Nottingham building was further than Randy anticipated on foot. He couldn't wait to hang out with his new friends. He finally arrived at the building.

Pierce and Emilio stood at the entrance, arms folded across their chest. "Hey, man!" They welcomed him into a large room loaded with electronics, computers, laptops, and other stolen things stacked along the brick wall. The Hillside Dominators seemed cool. Everyone wore a purple bandana and had a tattoo on their upper right cheek. Cigarette smoke filled the room. Pills and drug paraphernalia lay on the small table in a corner. Hours passed, it seemed the gang had no sense of timing. They were not in a hurry for any reason.

Sarah Rose finally crossed his mind. Two hours later, Randy verbalized that he needed to leave, his mom would be looking for him. Not to mention, he needed to call Sarah Rose. She and her family were different than Kerry Mitterson and her folks.

"Tomorrow night, we'll fill you in on our rules. Initiation is in three weeks," said Jody, eyeing several other new recruits standing near the wall, like prisoners lined up for chow.

"You have to go home to Momma, boy?" asked Emilio blowing circles of smoke in the air from his cigarette.

"Yeah," Randy replied. Laughter roared through the room.

"Don't worry, we'll toughen you up," Jody said.

He managed to creep into the apartment, tiptoe past his mom's room where he imagined she was sound asleep, and dialed Sarah Rose's cell number.

* * *

Phyllis nudged her cell phone lying beside her. I lit up, showing 10:30 p.m. *Must have been a really late meeting tonight,* she thought. She decided she'll talk to Randy in the morning. Phyllis made prior arrangements for a babysitter early in the week. She called Lea Robinsky who occasionally kept Chrissie when Meredith wasn't available.

"Gladly!" Lea exclaimed when Phyllis asked her to babysit Chrissie and Champion. "Enjoy your shopping excursion!" she added.

As the week flew by, the temp plummeted but Phyllis's spirits soared. She arose early Saturday morning and cooked a hearty breakfast for her family. Buttery pancakes, scrambled eggs, country sausages, and fruit energized them for the morning along with hot cocoa. Phyllis settled for a donut and a cup of coffee. Randy danced a two-step. Sarah agreed to go to the church carnival with him tonight. Phyllis dressed comfortably for shopping. She pulled on a light blue sweater over a pair of dark blue denim jeans. A navy blue peacoat kept her snug as she strolled out of the house to Lea's and meet Meredith afterward for their shopping excursion. Meredith had asked Phyll to meet her at Kirby's, one of Schenectady's upscale department stores. She questioned whether she was a teeny bit excited about seeing Brett again. She wasn't sure she was ready to honestly answer that question. She was certain she'd never fall in love again. Grayson had hurt her too deeply. She couldn't let that ever happen again.

Shoppers crammed the isles at Kirby's. "Phyll, look at this one," Meredith said, holding a vibrant printed dress against her body.

"Don't like it," said Phyllis. "It's too busy. A-line too. No, thanks."

They pulled dozens of dresses from the racks and moseyed to Malif's. They shopped at several other stores and finally went to Preve's where socialites shop. There they sifted through racks of dresses and trying them on.

"Wow, this one is really nice!" said Phyll. She pulled the yellow ruffle-back mermaid gown from the hanger. "Hurry, try it on! I can't wait to see it on you." Phyll excited handed it to her friend.

Meredith went into the dressing room and changed. She pranced in front of the full-length mirror as she modeled the strapless silk charmeuse dress. "I love it!" she said.

"It's a knockout," Phyll agreed. "Perfect for the banquet and ball on Saturday night. Oh, look!"

Meredith her Phyllis pointing to a black sequined dress on the next aisle. "It's simply gorgeous," said Meredith. "Try it on, Phyll."

Phyllis looked at the price tag. "Too expensive."

"Phyll, go ahead and try it on," Meredith urged. The sleeveless, asymmetrical crepe dress shouted elegance. "Phyll, you're gorgeous in that dress!"

Phyllis changed back into her clothes. Meredith took both of the signature gowns to the counter and paid for them with excitement. They left Preve excited about their lovely gowns and how they couldn't wait to wear them at the class reunion banquet and ball. As they entered the mall, the spicy smell of pizza hung in the air from the Italian shops.

Phyllis checked the time. "We've been shopping since 9:00 a.m. It's 12:45 p.m. Ready for lunch? It's on me," offered Phyl.

"Sure," said Meredith. "Madison's is on the upper level. They have the best calamari."

"Terrific," said Phyll, rubbing her stomach like a kid.

They chuckled at her lightheartedness and took the elevator to the fourth floor of the mall. Diners still filled rows of tables by the time Phyllis and Meredith reached Madison's. The bright red and silver décor gave the chic restaurant an air of opulence. A waiter seated them and handed both of them a menu. They giggled and chattered like girls at a sleepover. "Take your time looking at the menus. I'll be right with you," he said politely and whisked off to serve another table.

* * *

A gigantic planter stood in the corner of the room with giant green leaves waving their arms against a mirrored wall. Behind the planter, Grayson seated himself. He looked up in time to see the waiter lead Phyllis and Meredith three tables in front of his. He saw the waiter take their jackets and watched them place their orders. He gently set his coffee mug on the table and gazed in disbelief at his good luck. The waiter soon returned to serve them steaming hot entrees. He eyed Phyllis. *Now or never*, he thought. He'll talk to her about starting child support payments today. He decided to wait until she finished her meal. After all, he needed the time to build his nerves.

Grayson rose from his chair and walked over to their table. "Hello, Phyllis. How are you doing?" He glanced down at Meredith and gave her a tiny nod of his head.

Phyllis gazed up at Grayson as if she had seen a ghost. Speechless for a moment, then she pulled her hair back in a ponytail "What do you want?" she asked coldly.

"Regarding child support, I need one of your blank checks to set up a direct deposit into your account. I'm doing it this week. How are Randy and Chrissie?"

Phyllis gave him a blank stare. After some time, she wordlessly reached in her purse to pull out her checkbook. She tore out a blank check and gave it to him.

"Thanks," Grayson said as he strutted out the restaurant with his head down.

CHAPTER 14

"Transforming Lives and Building Generations," Saint Mark's slogan hung on a huge white banner in bold red letters across the front of the open field. The banner flapped back and forth in the brisk autumn breeze, welcoming all to the event that ranked second only to Schenectady's Walkabout Faire. Maple and dogwood trees had just begun to flame color. Their golden leaves danced wildly across an open field near the church.

Hey! Look out, you clowns!" Toby McPhie hollered from across the field with both arms flailing, eyeing a wagonload of teens. Peals of laughter and youthful chatter reverberated in the air. Several teenagers perched on bales of hay high-fived each other and sang tunes as the horse-drawn wagon creaked along the dirt path adjacent to the field. "Easy as pie." Toby opened his mouth as wide as a hippopotamus and plunged his head into a tin tub filled with apples bobbing on the surface.

Twins Brent and Braxton kept the hype going and dared him to dunk again. Randy and Sarah Rose joined Julie and another couple at the contest to watch Toby dunk his head into the tub of apples for the third time. Giggling like a kid, Toby shook himself like a drenched dog shaking its furry coat. He spit an apple from his mouth into his hand and took a large bite.

Sarah Rose stood too close to Toby that a spray of droplets landed at the corner of her mouth. A playful grin showed on her face as she licked it off, grinning at Randy. Randy leaned over and gave her a quick kiss on the forehead. They broke off from the crowd and took a walk together. Randy enjoyed her closeness. She was pretty. Her smile, her thoughtfulness, and her joy were many of her attributes he admired. They strolled along from one booth to another—holding hands; talking at times; and nibbling on corn dogs, candied apples, and other carnival goodies. They settled at a table of their own and exchanged ideas and small talk. Sarah Rose even talked about her relationship with the Lord. He looked at her now more affectionately than ever. She was only sixteen, but she was about God.

"How's your probation coming?" Sarah Rose asked.

"This is it. Setting up for the carnival today counts toward the last of my community service hours."

A gentle grin swept across her face. "Great!" She caressed Randy's hand.

"You're an angel, but what's this God's stuff? I mean, why does God mean so much to you?" he asked with an intense stare in her hazel eyes.

Sarah Rose sat straight up. "God cares for me, for you, and for the world. Who else has that kind of track record?" she asked, awaiting his response.

"You mean God cares for me?" asked Randy. A conversation about God felt strange but good all at the same time. In the short time he spent with her, he learned that Sarah Rose and her family were different than Kerry Mitterson and her folks. He liked the difference, but he wasn't ready for the God stuff yet. He had to admit that he liked Sarah Rose.

* * *

"Hey, man! We on for tonight? "I could do with a tall one."

"Sure thing." Randy high-fived Jody as he entered the dank Nottingham building, their hideout.

"Hey, you! Over here!" a familiar voice echoed across the room. Harry Lewis sat two seats over from Randy in their English class. Randy fist bumped Harry and showed a row of straight teeth.

"Listen up, everybody," said Jody, yanking a crumpled piece of paper from his light jacket engraved with the acronym HD. No one stirred. Total silence shrouded the room. "Tonight we begin initiation for our new Dominators."

In one movement, they waved the Dominator's bandana colors. Jody filled Randy, Harry, and another new gang member in on the Foster's Electrical Supply planned robbery. Initiation required several robberies and a big one at Farmer's Bank they had been working on for months.

"What about old man Givens?" Harry asked who was familiar with his neighbor's business.

"Yeah, what about him?" said Jody. "You mean if he gets in the way, don't you?" He grabbed Harry by the collar. "You just knock him off." The gang roared in laughter. Randy swallowed hard and made three short nods, returning Jody's gaze. "By the way," Jody said, turning in Randy's direction and lifted three strands of braids, "shave it off, bro." To the rest, he added, "Meet back here at nine o'clock. Thursday. No sloppy work."

* * *

On Monday morning, Phyllis strode into the office with a bounce in her step. She glanced at the line to the coffee pot. Lil, Karen, and Eloisa filled their cups and sipped from the brew, exchanging morning chatter. Phyllis made the usual cup of black coffee and turned her computer on. The workplace atmosphere was low key for a Monday morning. Then Rylander's e-mail hit her cold in the face, "All hands on deck. Meet me in the conference room at 8:30 a.m. sharp. WBR." Whenever Rylander signed a staff e-mail with all of his initials, it was not good news. William Barrett Rylander was not about to deliver a great-job-team speech, she surmised.

Fifteen minutes later, the crew marched into the main conference room liked trained zombies.

"We have a problem, a crisis of epic proportion," Rylander said, stroking his chin." The new 300-million-dollar contract with Smith Davidson and Sons fell through. Their executives said the problem is ours. We let the ball drop on this one. The Fontel project was a light-weight compared to our profits on this one. C'mon, people! What's the deal here?" he asked, his eyes searching around the table. "Stop everything you're working on and go back over every inch of contractual details. Check e-mails, check phone logs, and look at everything. I want a report same time tomorrow morning. Is that clear?"

"Yep!" Van Nieman and Wilson said in unison.

Everyone dashed out of the conference room to research the possible problems.

* * *

After work, on her way to Lil Tots, Phyllis turned the radio volume a little louder than normal to drown out Rylander's voice from the hectic meeting. It helped a little, but seeing Chrissie always took her troubles away. She strolled into the day care with joy.

"Hello, Mrs. Whitmore. How was your day?" Mrs. Glover greeted Phyllis.

"Great, thank you for asking." *If only she knew how chaotic the staff meeting had been, Mrs. Glover wouldn't ask*, she thought.

"Did Chrissie eat a heavy dinner last night?" Mrs. Glover asked. "She picked at her breakfast and ate a wee bite for lunch today. It's unusual for her."

"No, but I'm sure she's fine," assured Phyllis. "Toddlers go through stages in their diet. Thanks for letting me know. See you tomorrow." Phyllis gave Mrs. Glover a gentle hug as Chrissie waved good-bye to the other kids.

After leaving the day care, Phyllis drove to the closest grocery store, remembering she had to pick up milk and some other items. She opened the bank account app on her cell phone to view the checking account balance prior to shopping. Phyllis blinked, confused about the amount reflecting in the account. Could the bank have made a mistake? She did not have eight hundred dollars in the account last night. In fact, the account was pretty low with less than a hundred dollars. Phyllis called the bank.

"Which account would that be," asked the bank teller on the other end of the phone, "checking or savings?"

"Checking," Phyllis answered. A considerable increase in her account balance signaled that First Bank of Schenectady made an error. *Maybe it was a deposit from child support payment. Had it started?* She hoped for the latter.

"Looks like a deposit was made this morning from CSEO," said the personal banker.

"CSEO?" Phyllis questioned, raising an eyebrow.

"Child support enforcement office, ma'am. Child support payments are made via that office."

Phyllis heaved a sigh of relief and joy. She thanked the personal banker, ended the call, and paid for the groceries. Things were beginning to look up. She had the apartment for her family and now child support. "Thank you, Lord," she whispered.

* * *

Ding! The silver door of the elevator opened. Decked out like runway models, Phyllis and Meredith emerged from the elevator into Schenectady's new five-star hotel. The Omni radiated and buzzed with social events tonight. Phyllis's black gown looked svelte. They entered the ballroom, ready to mingle with the other classmates who would share in the joy of their twenty-first high school reunion. Phyllis dismissed the brief thought of seeing Brett. She tapped her toes to the soft romantic music that filled the lavish room. A huge crystal chandelier with gold accents hung midcenter. Silk ivory tablecloths draped over round tables with a gold charger placed at each setting. A large gold tieback perfectly accented the ivory chair covers. One small crystal bowl with a floral centerpiece and greenery commanded attention in the middle of the table, creating a total ambience of elegance.

"Fit for royalty, wouldn't you say?" Phyllis remarked her approval of the room's elegance. Meredith gave a single nod and checked the menu items. They headed toward the table where Zel sat with some of the other classmates who were seemingly enjoying themselves already.

"Hi there! Don't you girls look stunning?" Birdie said, dressed in a flaming red dress. Scanning Phyllis from head to toe, a smirk appeared at the corner of her mouth. She gave Phyllis a blank stare. "You still looking for a husband, Phyllis?" Then she whisked off into the crowd.

Phyllis's face went hot immediately. She heaved a long sigh and held back an angry outburst. Turning to Meredith, "Birdie needs something in her life," she said.

"Something?" Meredith countered. "More like *someone*—God."

Phyllis paused. "I hope she finds him soon."

She and Meredith paced to the table where Zel seated herself next to Paul Jamison, Dee Dee Mosley, and Charles Werner. Chatter and laughter spread around the center table. She and Meredith joined them and soon dived into sharing the joys of recollections, filling the atmosphere around the table with the air of good ole times.

Standing along the wall, nibbling on *hors d'oeuvres*, Brett Lancaster watched Phyllis from across the room.

Charles Werner immediately connected with Meredith. Meredith was not aware of Charles' previous romantic feelings for her. He heard about her husband's untimely death, but out of respect, he felt it was too soon to convey his feelings. He hoped tonight would change that since he had plans to see her again soon. Schenectady's economic status fit into his growing business, which involved opening several restaurants in Schenectady.

The band played one of the hottest hits. Paul Jamison nudged Zel for a dance. Charles Werner followed suit and escorted Meredith to the ballroom floor. Over her shoulder, he gave Phyllis a playful wink. Phyllis smiled back warmly at her friend in the warm yellow mermaid gown that matched her own mood tonight. Phyllis saw Brett Lancaster making a beeline for her. A flood of memories washed over her.

"You look gorgeous. May I please have this dance?" he asked, holding his right hand out to her.

Looking up into his eyes, Phyllis smiled and rose from the chair. "That would be great," she said.

Brett drew Phyllis close on the dance floor, enjoying the whiff of her perfume. "So how has life been treating you? How is Grayson?" Brett asked, noticing that she was not wearing a wedding ring. Phyllis's eyes searched his. Memories whirred in her mind, and her heart raced under his gaze. "I'm sorry, I don't mean to pry." His amiable smile faded.

"No, it's fine." She drew in a short breath and steeled herself. "Grayson and I are divorced. How are you and your family?"

"In a word, busy. I've been studying to earn a second doctoral degree. Work also keeps me pretty busy."

When the song ended, the couples returned to their seats as the waiters bustled like soldiers under orders to serve the scrumptious dinner of steak and lobster. Brett escorted Phyllis to her seat and sat beside her. Zel and Dee Dee focused on taking selfies on their cell phones. Phyllis enjoyed the hearty meal. Brett agreed that the crème brûlée and cheesecake were top notch.

Birdie's voice rang loud at the table behind them. Brett whirled around and caught her eye. Phyllis noticed his agitation and felt the heat rise in her own face. "Talk about being full, I can use some exercise. What do you say we work off some that cheesecake and go for a walk?" he suggested.

Phyllis eyed him for a brief moment. "A walk would be nice."

Brett pictured her mind weighing the idea. *Had he messed up again?* They exited the ballroom and found a quiet but lavishly decorated corner where a few couples were engaged in private conversations. Shortly after they were seated, Brett's cell phone rang.

"Please excuse me, I have to take this call…Yes, yes, I'm on my way," he answered the caller on the other end. Dr. Joliff, the head surgeon, was attending the annual medical conference in Chicago, Illinois. An emergency surgery required Brett, Dr. Joliff's assistant, to report to duty immediately. "I'm sorry, Phyllis. I must go. Call you later," he said and bolted to the nearest exit.

A quizzical expression crept across her face. Her eyes followed Brett to the exit.

CHAPTER 15

THE RUNDOWN NOTTINGHAM building was now home to two new gang members, Bo Viceroy and Ricky Bolden. Randy linked up with Pierce and Emilio, making the gang sign of the Hillside Dominators. Bo and Ricky knew little restraint. Both were outspoken but not for long.

"Hey, listen up." A serious look crossed Jody's pimpled face. "Time to get down to some real business. Tomorrow night at ten o'clock sharp, we knock off old man Givens. Everbody all in?"

Pierce immediately replied in his Guyanese dialect. The others roared in unison, throwing up the gang sign, "We're all in!"

"We'll pull off the big job as soon as a few more details get worked out. This time, the Dominators will go for the big bucks. We'll hit the Union Bank on the corner of Prospect and Turner Streets. Anybody get in the way, we blow them away," Jody said.

"Look, man, I just got out of the feds. I ain't going back. I'm not blowing *nobody* away!" Bo said in huff.

Jody's eyes widened. He punched Bo in the chest and then a hard blow against his cheeks. Randy, Pierce, Emilio, and Ricky hunkered along the wall close to the stolen items. Bo reeled back then straightened up. He clenched his fists up, hunched his shoulders, and spread his feet wide in a ready stance. Jody pounced, pushing him back against the wall and then to the grimy floor. Bo staggered up with a groan, brushed a hand across his bruised cheek, and then spit out some blood.

"Changed your mind?"

"Yeah," said Bo with a single nod of the head.

The room went silent, a calm before the storm. Randy drew in a ragged breath as his blood ran cold through his veins. The thought of hurting someone—correction, killing someone—cut through him. Like being punched in the chest, Jody's actions knocked the wind out of him.

* * *

Brett reviewed his thoughts and feelings as he sped his sleek black Mercedes along Riverside Boulevard toward the Children's Hospital of Schenectady. Looking at Phyllis tonight drew him back to their high school days when he had wanted to date her. Grayson beat him to the mark and latched on to her. The memory of her charismatic, good-natured character, and womanly attributes still checked all the boxes for him. It had been years since he had these feelings, but tonight they resurfaced in his heart. Was he ready to fall head over heels again after Carly? Was Phyllis even interested in more than a friendship? She had been reticent about her divorce. Something, however, passed between their glances. For a man who crossed women off his list for a long time, his actions tonight surprised him.

He pulled into his assigned parking space in front of the hospital and dashed toward the emergency room.

* * *

As Phyllis thought back to the events of the reunion, Brett's image settled over her. He still had a certain swagger that she always admired. He had the same trim muscular build at a towering six feet next to her five-foot-seven-inch frame.

The nostalgic expression faded from her face recalling Brett's abandonment. A myriad of questions remained. Why did he suddenly leave? He had not mentioned a wife. No woman in her right mind would pass him up. Grayson made a 180-degree turn. Her interest in men had vanished after her failing marriage and divorce. She reminded herself that her goal was to help Randy stay on track in life and take care of Chrissie. She felt abandoned and forlorn. She's convinced she didn't have time for men. She couldn't be true to herself and trust in a relationship again?

* * *

Weeks later, the mercury barely rose when October sneaked in with unusually cool temperatures. However, the levels between Meredith and Charles Werner signaled a heat wave. Meredith reflected on the recent events in her life. Lately she had an additional pep in her step. Charles Werner called her at least once a week since their recent hookup at the reunion. A call from Phyllis interrupted her thoughts as she pulled into her driveway.

"Hello, Phyll. Come on in."

Phyllis entered Meredith's home and immediately embraced her in a bear-hug. When she released Meredith, she whirled around to see dozens of red, white, and pink roses in a crystal vase tied with a lovely pink bow. Phyllis scampered over to the mosaic table and inhaled the fragrant flowers. "Let me guess, Charles Werner?" she asked.

"Uh-huh," replied Meredith in a soft tone.

"Congratulations! No one is more deserving of happiness than you."

"Phyll, update me on Brett. What's he up to these days?"

A pensive look showed on Phyllis's face. She answered Meredith in a reflective tone. "He told me that he's quite busy continuing his education. Said he's about to start a new venture at work. I didn't get a chance to ask about his occupation, just that he was enjoying his work."

A pleasant expression showed on Meredith's face.

* * *

A little after 9:30 p.m., Randy pulled on a light jacket and hurried to the Nottingham building. His thoughts bounced around in his head. He did not look forward to knocking off old man Givens or anyone else, for that matter. He drew an imaginary line on that thought. However, he could not appear weak. Hillside Dominators do not take well to weaklings or quitters. Old man Givens and the Hillside Dominators had their previous run-ins. Jody, the leader of the gang, aimed to fix this tonight. "Let's go," he hollered to Pierce, Bo, Ricky, Randy, and some of their other gang members.

A scrolling neon sign flashed Givens Electronics across the front of the brick building. Pierce provoked Jess Givens, the owner, many times in his shop. Jody watched from across the dimly lit street and told the guys to take their posts as they had discussed. Jody had a clear-cut view through the glass entrance and the side view.

Unbeknownst to the gang, an eagle-eyed policeman in plainclothes and Mammoth, his killer dog, was hunkered out of sight in an unmarked car. He had been informed about the gang's activity. From his angle, he could see their movement without discovering him. The rest of the gang took their places on either side of the building, away from the side door. Randy and Bo stood close to the entrance, unaware of the security camera. The policeman recognized his face from a previous camera shot. He moved in calmly when he saw Pierce open the door and made a beeline to the counter where Givens was preparing to close shop for the night. Mammoth was not so calm. His ferocious bark rang in the air. "Good boy!" the policeman stroked the oversized dog as they entered the shop.

Pierce reached over the counter and grabbed Givens by the collar. He did not see the policeman or Mammoth until the dog growled fiercely and pounced his chest. After a scuffle, two giant paws knocked him to the tile floor.

"You're under arrest!" the policeman yelled and clamped two shiny bracelets on Pierce's wrist.

Jody and the rest of the gang scattered like chickens getting away from a junkyard dog.

* * *

Monday morning, Phyllis arrived late at Lil Tots Daycare. She noticed that Chrissie did not display the usual excitement. After signing the daily log, Phyllis planted a kiss on Chrissie's curly head then exited the building.

"Have a nice day." Mrs. O'Neil waved Phyllis good-bye then walked Chrissie to her class.

On the way to the office, she reflected on Chrissie's unusual behavior. She drank less than a few ounces of milk for breakfast. Was she overreacting concerning her daughter? Like the mix of peanut butter and jelly, toddlers and picky eaters go together.

Later that afternoon, Chrissie fainted on the playground during recess. Trisha Baldwin, Mrs. O'Neil's youthful assistant, sprinted into the hallway toward the director's office.

What's wrong?" The director asked after hearing Trisha's frantic voice.

"It's Chrissie Whitmore, she fainted! She passed out in the playground tumblers."

Minutes later, a wailing siren of an ambulance turned into Lil Tots' driveway. The office assistant called Phyllis. After Phyllis calmed down, she informed Mrs. Glover that she'd meet the ambulance at the hospital. On the way to Children's Hospital of Schenectady, her cell phone rang.

"Hello, Ms. Whitmore? This is Mr. Claremont."

Maybe he is calling to confirm Randy's community service hours or make some other plans with him, she thought. "Hello, how are you, Mr. Claremont?"

"I'm afraid I'm doing better than you—or better than your son, I should say." Phyllis raised an eyebrow. Her chest rose and fell as she let out a long, exasperated sigh. "Randy's in big trouble. We need to talk, ma'am. Can you come to my office this evening or in the morning?"

"Tomorrow morning perhaps," she managed to say in a clear voice. My youngest child is in an emergency. As we speak, I'm heading to the hospital's emergency room. I'll contact you tomorrow."

"Fine, ma'am, but please make sure you call me."

Her hopes were dashed into pieces. Disheartened, tears welled up and spilled down both cheeks. She cupped her mouth to control the sobbing with one hand while keeping the other on the steering wheel. A truck on the outer lane honked as the Lexus swerved too close to it. She rammed her foot to the pedal and accelerated. Minutes later, the hospital came into view. She parked her car and tore out of it toward the emergency room entrance. Phyllis rushed around the winding corridors toward the emergency room. Fear rippled through her body as she rounded the corners. The smell of bleach floated in the air where a janitor had cleaned a spill. Phyll reached the end of the long hallway and turned left for a short distance.

* * *

With a stethoscope slung around his neck, Brett strode to Chrissie's bed and began to examine the toddler shortly before Phyllis reached the room.

"Vitals all taken," said one of the nurses as she handed Dr. Brett Mooreland Chrissie's medical chart.

Another nurse who had been listening to Chrissie's heart rhythm straightened and placed the stethoscope in the pocket of her white lab coat. Brett immediately began to examine Chrissie who was still dazed.

Phyllis dashed to curtain number 21 of the emergency room and ran to Chrissie's side. As soon as she saw Chrissie, her legs buckled. She grabbed the rail for support. Steadying herself, she leaned over the bed and enveloped Chrissie in a fleeting hug. A nurse pushing a monitor opened the curtain.

"I'm Dr. Moreland," Brett said, laying a calming hand on hers. For a very brief moment, a quizzical look was etched on her face. Brett recalled that he did not get a chance to tell her about his job in Schenectady or his position at the hospital. "We'll take good care of her. We must run some test," he said, escorting Phyllis to the chair in the corner. "It looks like we may have to admit Chrissie."

Phyllis blinked in disbelief.

CHAPTER 16

CHRISSIE'S FEVER SPIKED by the hour. Like a father expecting his first child, Phyllis paced the floor back and forth. A woman from the admissions office interrupted her midstride when she requested Chrissie's insurance coverage. Phyllis searched her purse. Then she remembered that Grayson carried the family's health coverage through his job. She had forgotten to get the health insurance cards from him. She had to call him.

Later that morning, Brett reviewed Chrissie's X-rays. Appendicitis. He would have to perform emergency surgery. He discussed the procedure with her. In spite of the situation, seeing Phyllis today lifted him into the clouds.

"Thanks, Bret—I mean, Dr. Moreland," she said in a choked whisper.

Brett laid a comforting hand over hers then he left quickly to prepare for emergency surgery. Phyllis's mind swirled with anxiety before the surgery began. She stepped out of the room and found the hospital chapel. She needed time pray and to reflect alone. The tranquil atmosphere of the small room helped to calm her as she rehearsed the events that had darkened her day. Brett had assured her that Chrissie would be okay, which raised her hopes up. She chided herself for not paying closer attention to Chrissie. She was grateful that Brett would perform the surgery, but his position at the hospital surprised her. *Why didn't he tell her?* she wondered

A couple of hours later, the surgery went well. Phyllis stayed at her side while Chrissie recovered. The next day, Phyllis called Mr. Claremont and explained her situation again. She would not leave Chrissie's bedside, she informed him.

"I'm sorry to hear of your daughter's illness, Mrs. Whitmore, but we must meet and talk about your son. How about Friday 3:00 p.m.?|

"That's fine. I'll see you then."

On Thursday morning, giggles could be heard in Chrissie's room. Brett was standing beside Phyllis next to Chrissie's hospital bed as they watched her sitting upright on the bed and slurping chocolate ice cream from a cone. He smiled widely at the child's ice cream mustache. She promised to save some of the ice cream for Champion. Phyllis smiled and tousled Chrissie's curly locks. A look of relief was pasted on her face. Phyllis reached down and planted a kiss on Chrissie's forehead, leaving an imprint of her red lipstick.

Brett studied the tender moments between mother and daughter with a twinkle in his eyes. Phyllis thanked him for his help. He enveloped her in a brief-hug. As his steady gaze bore into her soul, her heart skipped a beat. Brett scribbled notes on Chrissie's med chart and placed it under his arm. A loud voice over the intercom announced, "Dr. Moreland, room 210. Stat."

He gave Phyllis a wink. "I look forward to seeing you soon," he said and sprinted to room 210. Phyllis watched him leave the room, a sweet smile crossed her face.

"For Champion," Chrissie said, handing Phyllis the messy stub of the ice cream cone she almost finished. Phyllis let out a soft chuckle.

On Friday evening, a fine drizzle turned into a heavy downpour. Phyllis had the meeting with Mr. Claremont. *What had Randy done now? Hadn't she monitored him more closely?* She grounded him as punishment, which included no dating. Like the downpour outside, trouble poured down in torrents.

"Young man, do you realize the gravity of your situation?" Mr. Claremont asked Randy. He swiveled his chair around and faced

Phyllis. "Ms. Whitmore, Randy is a member of a gang, the Hillside Dominators. If convicted, he could go to prison."

"Gang? Prison?" Phyllis gasped, cupping both hands over her mouth. She stood up too quickly from her seat, making her feel wobbly like a young colt standing on his legs for the first time.

Next to Mr. Claremont, the arresting officer stood up and said, "Randy Whitmore, the Hillside Dominators will no longer dominate this area or any other territory. They're going down. Unless you cooperate with us, you are too." Randy fidgeted with both hands, his head lowered.

Phyllis sighed. "What can we do?" she asked the officer desperately.

"Ma'am, Randy must help himself," the officer said. Where is his father? We'd like to talk to him as well." A hush fell over the room for a moment. The officer moved over to Randy and placed a finger under his chin, tilting it upward. "We're going to get *all* of the Dominators," he declared as Randy's eyes met his.

A heavy weight crushed Phyllis' chest. She wanted to run away. Her trouble left her wondering. *Is it possible to live sane in a chaotic world?*

CHAPTER 17

MAGGIE SULLIVAN'S VOICE echoed in Phyllis mind when she awakened early Saturday morning, "Come soon, and bring the children." She promised Granny Mag that they would visit soon. A trip, especially now, would be good for her sanity and health. Phyllis decided to make the trip since Meredith had been gracious to keep Chrissie and Randy. The two-hour drive would help remove some of the stress and find some clarity in her thoughts. She could not wait to see her beloved grandmother.

Two hours later, Phyllis drove past the Farmers' Museum and the National Baseball Hall of Fame in Cooperstown, New York. Soon she pulled up the gravel driveway. A gray picket fence surrounded the yard that enclosed the winding porch. When she got out of the car, Duke and Dudley, Granny Mag's golden retrievers, nuzzled her legs, begging to be petted. Phyllis stooped down and stroked the dogs as they barked.

Hearing Duke and Dudley barking outside, Granny put down the novel she had been reading on the small table beside the sofa and peered out the window. Hearing Phyllis's voice outside the door banged, she quickly opened the door with outstretched arms. After they exchanged a warm hug, Granny said, "It's good to see you. I didn't think you'd darken this door anytime soon. Come into the house, it's a little nippy outside." Granny looked around, searching for Randy and Chrissie. "Where are the children? Are you all right?" she asked in a single breath "I was just indulging in cup of coffee and teacakes while I finished a chapter of the novel I'm reading." Inside the red brick house set in the middle of historic farmland, Granny Mag poured Phyllis a cup and placed a plate of lemony teacakes in front of her.

Phyllis took a seat across from Granny at the kitchen table and reminisced about the early part of her childhood in Cooperstown. The same yellow walls displayed various family photos. At Granny's home, the dark hardwood floors glistened as always. The cheerful and cozy atmosphere still lingered in the immaculate home. Phyllis studied her grandmother's face a moment, the classic lines, a well-sculpted nose, wide-set eyes as brown as walnuts, a full mouth that always curved upward into a pleasant grin, and her mother's features in her grandmother's face. She admired her grandmother's sweet spirit and beauty.

"Something wrong, Phyll?" She could always read Phyllis like the daily newspaper.

She drew in a lengthy breath. "You could say that," she said, brushing away a lone tear that trailed down her cheek. Cradling a large coffee mug with both hands, she filled Granny Mag in on all of the happenings and incidents that weighed her down.

Mag, as she was affectionately called by her neighbors, stared long and hard into her eyes, shaking her head and nodding several times out of concern. She sat next to Phyllis. "I love you so much, I hope you know that," Granny Mag said as she stroked her granddaughter's face, her own eyes glistening with tears. She gently pulled Phyllis to face her squarely. "Phyllis, do you know what I see?" Granny asked.

"No," Phyllis responded with reverence. "What do you see Granny? Please tell me."

Granny Mag smiled broadly. "I see a grand opportunity, my dear. Do you understand?"

"No, I don't think I do." Phyllis searched Granny's eyes intently.

"Phyllis, my dear, I want you to know that man's extremity is God's opportunity. You have an opportunity to allow God to show Himself strong on your behalf." She held Phyllis's chin in her hand.

"Will you go with me to church tomorrow? We have a great pastor, and his messages are inspirational and truly encouraging."

"I'd love to go," Phyllis said, holding Granny Mag close.

They embraced each other for a long while and stepped into the living room to continue their heart-to-heart talk. They shared story after story until Granny Mag let out a long yawn.

"I'm sorry, dearie, you must be exhausted from the long drive. You should get some sleep. Phyll, have a good night. I'll see you in the morning." She added, "A friendly reminder, dearie, breakfast is served early around here." She let out another yawn and padded to her bedroom.

"Good night, Granny Mag, and pleasant dreams to you as well," Phyllis said. A soft chuckle escaped her as she watched her mosey down the hall to the bedroom. Phyllis wondered what exhaustion looked like on Granny, now she knew.

Phyllis tossed in bed, agitated and wrestling with her thoughts. A sense of guilt pervaded her mind of not attending church. Today she had been reminded by Granny's invitation. Without realizing it, the invite was a subtle reminder that attending and participating in church service was the right thing to do. After all, hadn't Granny taught her that early in life. She could not remember the last time she attended a church service since she had been married. Neither she nor Grayson participated in religious activities.

At seven thirty the next day, Granny and Phyllis finished the breakfast dishes and got dressed for church. Saint Luke's Church abounded with the fervor of parishioners greeting each other on Sunday morning. Maggie and Phyllis walked up the travertine pathway and entered the foyer of the church.

"Hello, Mrs. Sullivan," one of the parishioners greeted Granny Mag.

"Mrs. Aikman, how are you today? This is my granddaughter, Phyllis," Granny said with every ounce of cheer she could muster. Her love and pride for Phyllis showed.

Phyllis and Granny exchanged greetings with several parishioners before seating themselves. The congregation rose and words flashed on the screen on either side of the podium. The arms of the people attending the service lift up in praise as music and words blended harmonically into a joyful medley. An organ sat opposite the piano on the left side of the church. The musician on the piano and the organ both played skillfully.

> *What a Friend we have in Jesus, all of our sins and griefs to bear. O what needless pain we bear, all because we do not carry everything to God in prayer.*

The words resonated in Phyllis's mind. The choir then sang in unison.

> *Shackled by a heavy burden, 'neath a load of guilt and shame. Then the hand of Jesus touched me, And now I am no longer the same. He touched me. Oh, He touched me, and oh the joy that floods my soul! Something happened and now I know, He touched me and made me whole.*

Reverend Barker, a lanky man with gray sideburns, stood at the podium. He welcomed everyone with warmth and kindness. After a short introduction of the sermon, Reverend Barker asked everyone to stand. "Please turn your Bibles to the New Testament passage in 1 Peter 5:10." He began to read:

> *And the God of all grace, who called you to his eternal glory in Christ, after you have suffered a little while, will himself restore you and make you strong, firm and steadfast. To him be the power forever and ever. Amen.* (1 Peter 5:10 NIV)

"Do you hear the hope and assurance of these promises? Hope for tomorrow and the assurance of a brighter future. That offer is yours personally," Reverend Barker's booming voice echoed. His eyes scanned the large crowd and locked eyes with Phyllis. "We're God's precious children so why does He allow us to get hurt, take loved ones, or let loved ones leave us? How can any of us stay sane in this crazy, mixed up, and chaotic world? This passage says even when we suffer, we're blessed because we have hope in Jesus. We suffer because Christ suffered for us. We have hope in Jesus. We're to keep our eyes turned to Him, and He will comfort us and give us strength. In the Old Testament, Isaiah 26:3 assures us of God's peace that helps us to obtain and keep our sanity in this life.

> *He will keep in perfect and constant peace the one whose mind is steadfast [that is, committed and focused on Jesus—in both inclination and character], Because he trusts and takes refuge in You [with hope and confident expectation].* (Isa. 26:3 AMP)
>
> *Then you will experience God's peace, which exceeds anything we can understand. His peace will guard your hearts and minds as you live in Christ Jesus.* (Phil. 4:7 NLT)

"Let's examine the matter further," said Reverend Barker. "Did you know that God feels what we feel? Hebrews 4:15 tells us:

> *For we have not a high priest which cannot be touched with the feeling of our infirmities; but was in all points tempted like as we are, yet without sin.* (Heb. 4:15 KJV)

"Imagine that God feels your pain along with you. He also knows the intensity of your pain and will not load you down with more burdens than He has enabled you to carry. One more thing, it is a fact that God catches every one of your tears and collects them in a bottle of remembrance." Reverend Barker again read from the Bible.

> *You keep track of all my sorrows. You have collected all my tears in your bottle. You have recorded each one in your book.* (Ps. 56:8 NLT)

"Can you imagine that? God cares so much about your pain that He catches every tear you shed to remind Himself to limit your sufferings. I want to remind you that the Lord will not allow you to suffer more than you can handle."

During the service, Phyllis's spirits lifted as the pastor spoke. She tried to grasp and connect with everything he was saying. She was captivated by the scriptures. She closed her eyes and silently whispered a prayer for God to come into her heart. She softly prayed for God to become a genuine part of her life. She wanted a real inner change. An unprecedented sense of peace washed over her. For the first time, she felt a genuine connection with God and basked in His divine presence that had enveloped her soul. She would read those scriptures, but she didn't even own a Bible. That would change today. Granny had several Bibles, she'd ask her for one. Phyllis opened her eyes, straightened, and clasped Granny Mag's hand who gently squeezed her hands.

During the drive back to Schenectady, Brett's image came into Phyllis's mind. She recalled their last conversation at the hospital. He found her in the chapel and briefly shared his faith in God. Not only had his position at Children's Hospital surprised her, but his faith in God was equally amazing. He called her a loving and devoted mother and asked to see her again soon. Perhaps she could learn something deeper about God from him. When she nailed it all down, she admired Brett. But hadn't she vowed to never trust again? Never to love again?

* * *

Brett's day got off to an earlier start than normal for a Monday morning. Before heading to the emergency room, he sipped on a large cup of coffee that he hoped would fully wake him up. He sat quietly, pouring over his thoughts in the hospital cafeteria. Phyllis's delicate frame crossed his mind. He hoped to continue the old friendship they had started in college before Grayson came into the picture. For so many years, he fought the dream of being in a relationship with Phyllis. Carly, a lovely vivacious girl, and Brett dated through much of high school. They believed they were in love at one time. Later, he discovered that Carly had goals that went far beyond the small town of Schenectady. After graduation, she packed up and headed for college as a theater major, planning one day to move to Hollywood and try for her big break as an actress. Brett remembered how Carly shattered his dreams. The relationship ended, and he was hurt. He never wanted that to happen again.

At first, the idea of coming home to Schenectady felt like a step backward. When a friend of his mentioned the position that he now holds at the Children's Hospital had opened up in Schenectady, he immediately rejected the idea. He wasn't interested in returning to the little town he so eagerly fled, but the chance to escape the pain of his broken marriage with Carly and the opportunity to start life over changed his mind. He embraced the opportunity and made the move.

* * *

Phyllis returned home, basking in a wave of happiness with her spirits soaring. Seeing Chrissie play with Champion made her emotional state rise even higher. She breathed a sigh of relief seeing her toddler back to normal, eating right, and playing around again. She lifted her head and sent a thankful prayer to God. In retrospect, she and Randy would have a long talk. This time, she'd try to show more sensitivity to him. Perhaps she had been too hard on him. She gave Randy permission to connect with Sarah Rose again, which put his head in the clouds. *Was her hard shell the reason her son had been acting out?* she wondered.

* * *

Randy left school with a spring in his steps. His mother had taken him off punishment since he agreed to cooperate with the police. He wanted to call Sarah Rose and clear the air with her. Sarah Rose was a no-nonsense person that he truly cared about deeply.

While ambling down the long hallway at Schenectady High, Randy and Sarah Rose stopped by her locker on the way to the cafeteria to grab her science and math books. Randy spilled the beans about his run-in with the law. He spoke hesitantly about the Hillside Dominators but explained why he had not called and had been out of touch with her.

Sarah Rose scowled. She slammed the locker door where she was taking out a couple of books and turned to face him. "You need to turn things around in your life." She gave him a head-to-toe scan. "Randy, you've got make better choices, better decisions."

Squirming sideways, he admitted, "I didn't use good sense. The gang is a done deal. It's over." His tone was repentant.

"You must give your life to Jesus," she told him. "He alone fills the void in life. You must make a change. I...I won't accept anything less of you."

Randy froze. Silence hung in the air for a moment. Maybe there was truth in Sarah Rose's words. Randy contemplated the meaning of her words but he didn't know how to deal with the reality of it. Speechless, he stared into Sarah Rose's hazel eyes.

"What's the matter, cat got your tongue?" she asked. Sarah Rose felt half anger, half pity for Randy.

"I want to believe—I really do, but I don't know if I can," Randy said, taking her hands.

She cocked her head and glanced up at him. "In time, you'll believe."

They held hands and continued walking toward the cafeteria.

* * *

Like her friend Phyllis, Meredith also felt the wave of happiness. Things were going her way on every level. She reclined in the wingback chair in the living room, admiring the most recent floral arrangement she received from James Werner. Although she loved the attention, if he didn't stop flooding her with flowers, she would soon have to open a florist shop. The phone rang and redirected her reflection.

"Meredith, this is Mrs. Creighton. How are you? As you know, it's that time of year when we count on you to make your goodies for Oktoberfest. The event is a little over a week away. Your cookies always go over well. Can we depend on you for several dozen?"

"Of course. My pleasure as always," Meredith said in a pleasant voice. "I've been quite busy lately. Thank you for the friendly reminder."

"Great, and thank you. Now I must call Phyllis, dearie. Take care. I'll see you there. Bye."

Lightheartedly, Meredith strode into the kitchen as soon as Mrs. Creighton's telephone call ended. The slightest whiff of cinnamon hung in the air from a recent batch of oatmeal cinnamon cookies. Her soprano notes rang in the air while she hummed a tune as she searched the cupboards for the ingredients to be included on a revised shopping list. A smile lit up her face as she thought about Werner's Bakery that would soon open in Schenectady. Charles Werner had been a bright spot in her life since they reunited at their class reunion. He had become a fixture in her life, and she thanked God for his blessing.

* * *

Phyllis just hung up the phone with Mrs. Creighton concerning the Oktoberfest. It seemed like déjà vu since minutes before she received Mrs. Creighton's call, Brett phoned and invited her to attend the festival with him. After a back and forth of why she couldn't accept his invitation, Brett's argument won out, and she finally consented. It was time for new chapters, he told her. It was true a new chapter had begun. Hadn't she connected more with God? The new chapter was all about her transformation. How would Randy react? Would he accept any man other than his father, although Grayson walked out on them? She noticed he frowned when he overheard their phone conversation.

Brett called to inquire about Chrissie's well-being since she had been released from the hospital. Transitions had not only happened in her life but the weather changed as well. The temperature dropped drastically into the mid-fifties feeling more like November than the usual October temps. She looked forward to the outing with Brett and dressed themselves in warm garb. When Brett arrived at her apartment, excitement hung in the air. She and Chrissie both were like anxious kids the night before Christmas. As expected, Randy pouted. It was evident from his actions that Brett did not meet his approval. Randy and Sarah Rose went ahead of Brett and Phyllis to the Stockade district with two of their classmates, Matt and Bebe.

The historic Stockade swelled with crowds of people celebrating their heritage and enjoying Oktoberfest. Everyone joined in *Funtober*, the moniker for Oktoberfest, because of its acclaimed fun and excitement. The whirling waters of the Mohawk River induced déjà vu as Phyllis watched its swift foamy waters from the window of Brett's car. The river's winding streams curved past the Stockade district where her Dutch Colonial home used to exist. Memories gone by, she reminded herself. *Today is a brand-new day, and I'm a brand-new me.* She put her chin up and waited for Brett to park the Mercedes. He pulled into a space directly in front of the main entrance of an expansive brick building. Brett got out of the car and opened the door for her.

"Here we go," he said and glanced around at the crowd for a quick moment. An air of excitement hung around him.

Phyllis thanked him and then helped Chrissie out of the child seat. She took Chrissie with one hand while Brett held the other. Phyllis scrutinized the crowd and noted the several vendors that lined the streets. A gentle but cold breeze stirred as they strode toward the entrance of the brick building. Phyllis inhaled the aroma of the foods as the blast of Italian and other sausages sizzling on an open grill mingled with the cinnamon wafting from freshly baked apple pies in the breeze. Many people sipped on hot apple cider, nibbled on candied apples, and partake of every food item imaginable. She and Brett stopped at a table that displayed the various cultural items. Activities included pumpkin carvings, card games, and apple bobbing despite the cooler temperature. Every inch of a wide variety of pumpkins were decorated it seemed. Local farm produce were on many of the tables. A live band played while teenagers bobbed and weaved to the music.

When Phyllis and Brett entered the foyer, she noted that many of the activities were replicated. Friendly farmers featured farm-fresh fruits and vegetables, homemade items, flowers, and plants. An assortment of fall recipe cookbooks and Oktoberfest hats, lion-crested with German and other cultural motifs, filled some of the tables. Warm smiles from the large crowd of familiar faces gave the event inside a cozy warm feeling. A DJ played country music that filled the room, and couples danced the two-step across the wooden floor.

A man whose belly plopped over his belt shouted above the music and chatter of the crowd. "All aboard for hay rides through these doors." Phyllis spotted Randy and Sarah Rose seated on a stone bench, squirting mustard on their corn dogs. Having seen them, she could relax better. "Right this way," the man said.

Brett stepped back to allow Phyllis to move in front of him as they followed the man through the doorway. Phyllis leaned against Brett, tucking her head against his chest. Chrissie tagged alongside Phyllis, licking a lollipop that Phyllis had tucked away in her purse.

"Mommy, a Cinderella pumpkin!" screamed Chrissie, grunting as he tried to lift one on the hay near the doorway.

Brett smiled at Phyllis. She returned his smile with her soft chuckle. "You're the cute Cinderella," he said, hoisting Chrissie high up in his arms.

Phyllis guided them to a booth where toddlers were getting sparkly pink stickers. Brett plastered one on Chrissie's hand, which earned him a hug from her. Then they strode outside to join the hay riders on the horse-drawn wagons who were laughing and enjoying the fun and excitement of the festival.

CHAPTER 18

SEVERAL DAYS FOLLOWING the Octoberfest, Randy sat on the school bus, musing. Hanging out with Sarah Rose at the festival had been a hit. A tiny smile flickered at the corner of his mouth as he reflected on their growing relationship. Then Brett's image crossed his mind. Suddenly, his face puffed like a blowfish. His mother had discussed her and Brett's new relationship. It peeved him. No dope could take his dad's place, he thought. How would he handle this? He swiped his phone and dialed Grayson's cell number.

"Hello, son. How are you and Chrissie?" Grayson asked with chagrin.

"Uh, all right," Randy replied. "Dad, can we talk?"

"I can't leave my workplace. Can you come over to my office tomorrow?"

"Yeah."

"Take care, son. I'll see you in my office."

Randy secretly wished his dad would come back home and make things okay again. The next evening, Randy met Grayson in his office.

"Hello, son," he said, wrapping his arms around Randy. "What's up?" Grayson asked, staring at a reflection of himself in Randy. They had the same square shoulders and brown eyes. "Sit down," he said, pointing at the wing back chair facing his desk.

Randy plopped on the chair and wasted no time sharing his thoughts. He spilled the beans about Brett and Phyllis's relationship. Then he asked the pointed question, "Dad, can you come back home?"

Grayson winced, sitting behind the cherrywood desk. He tried to force meaningful words through his throat. He did not look forward to this meeting and was not ready to deal with any unsettled issues. Randy noticed his dad's unsettled emotions and leaned his lanky body forward, staring intently into his father's eyes without blinking.

Grayson finally responded. "Son, your mom has outgrown me, and she deserves more than I can offer her," he said in a less than congenial voice.

Randy released a ragged sigh and rolled his eyes to the ceiling for a brief moment. Feeling exasperated, he leaped out of his chair and bolted out of the office. Quick as lighting, he exited the building, plucked a cigarette from his pocket, and lit it. All he ever wanted was his father's total acceptance, family unity, and a meaningful family experience. The weight of anger and pain had caused his self-centeredness.

* * *

After a hard day of work without lunch, Brett stopped at the Jamaican cuisine restaurant for a hearty dinner. He decided to order curried goat over rice and vegetables with a sun-dried tomato-and-cucumber salad and a tumbler of iced tea. His thoughts played wildly in his mind. Not wanting to marry again, what was he doing establishing a relationship with Phyllis? He couldn't get her off his mind. He cared about Phyllis a lot. He enjoyed her company that day at the October festival and relished the opportunity to spend more time with her. Chrissie was cute and cuddly and added a spark to life. They talked and laughed for much of the evening. By the end of the day, Phyllis invited him to Thanksgiving dinner. His pulse skipped with anticipation. He cared about her more than he could admit. He chided himself, why play with the truth? He'd fallen in love with her again!

A strong cold breeze rattled the windows in the cramped kitchen as Phyllis searched the cupboards, trying to decide on their evening meal. The icy temperature coupled with the frigid wind helped her decide to make Randy and Chrissie's favorite soup, sandwiches, and apple pie for dessert. After a short while, the aroma of beef noodle soup wafted throughout the small apartment. As she began to trim slices of honey-baked ham, she heard a gentle knock on the door. She dabbed her hands quickly on the kitchen towel and strolled into the living room. She made a narrow opening in the door. Her expression changed immediately. Brett stood there, smiling.

"Hi. I hope you don't mind me dropping by without calling."

"No, not at all." Phyllis stepped back, opening the door wider. "Come in. Actually, I'm glad you stopped by." She motioned him inside, and he followed her to the kitchen. She reached for his coat and hung it in the hall closet. Brett bent and planted a gentle kiss on Phyllis's cheek. Her cheeks reddened and her eyes sparkled as she looked up at him. In a playful mood, Phyllis said, "Here you go, Chef." She handed Brett an apron.

He smiled. After washing his hands, he began peeling potatoes Phyllis gave him. Standing beside Brett in the kitchen felt perfect. Just two people laughing, talking about everyday things, and enjoying each other's company. Chrissie sat at the table, totally engaged in scribbling and coloring a turkey cutout her teacher had given her as homework.

"Brett would you set the table please?" Phyllis asked.

"Sure thing, Teeny," he said, winking.

"Teeny?" She slapped his shoulder playfully with the kitchen towel. "You remembered! I haven't heard that nickname since high school. Yeah, I suppose I was teeny tiny in those days." Phyllis poked her index finger in his chest playfully. "Get busy. Plates are in the cabinet above your head."

Laughter and chatter filled the room as they prepared dinner before Randy entered the kitchen. Randy soon came into the apartment on a high note. "Hey, Mom," he greeted Phyllis and headed straight for the fridge as usual. When he turned on his heels, he saw the back of Brett at the sink. He muttered discontent under his breath and leaned against the wall with his arms folded across his chest. Then he rolled his eyes to the ceiling, watching Brett pull out plates.

"Hello, Randy. How are you?" Brett spoke in a welcoming manner.

Randy ignored Brett, served himself, and then sat at the opposite end of the table close to Chrissie. He began to eat the hearty meal silently. Brett sent Phyllis an understanding look. She nodded in appreciation of his patience.

"Aren't you going to eat with us?" Phyllis asked Brett.

Brett shook his head. "Just coffee please. And maybe a tiny slice of apple pie later," he said, rubbing his full stomach.

After they had all eaten and the plates were cleared, Phyllis removed the apple pie from the oven and the vanilla ice cream from the freezer. When Phyllis placed a slice in front of Randy, he jumped out of the chair and dashed into his room, fuming.

Chrissie tried to ease the tension in the room. She darted to Brett and handed him the paper, a colored pencil, and drawing. "I write," she said.

"Angel, thank you," Brett said. He picked her up, put Chrissie on his lap, and scooted closer to Phyllis. Together they studied the squiggles and scribbles that was supposed to be a stick figure of Phyllis and Brett. Brett's heart exploded in love. He always wanted children. He gave her a big hug.

* * *

The time passed. October turned into November fast. Phyllis and Brett's relationship continued to grow over the weeks. She never guessed the difference it would make having Brett as a close personal friend, not just a classmate. His values and personality fit so well, and his love for children was evident. She had to admit that she needed him. Perhaps, in some ways, she felt that he needed her. She clung to Brett, not wanting to let go, but also afraid of hanging on. She couldn't be selfish and sacrifice Randy for a relationship, not even with Brett. It wouldn't be fair. He deserved better.

Thanksgiving plans had been settled over a week ago. Granny Mag invited her and the kids to come to the farm. Phyllis told Granny about her invitation for Brett to share Thanksgiving with them. She hoped Granny would agree to have Brett join them. "The more, the merrier," Granny Mag had said. "Have love and will share." Granny had such joy in her voice.

On the evening before Thanksgiving, Brett and Phyllis sat on the sofa in her living room. "Tomorrow is Thanksgiving," Brett said holding Phyllis in a sweet embrace. He searched her eyes. "Let's use that day to thank God for our reunion."

Returning Brett's gaze, Phyllis nodded and said, "But especially to thank God for salvation. For everything." Phyllis gently rested her head on his chest, recalling the words of Reverend Barker's life-changing sermon.

> *He will keep in perfect and constant peace the one whose mind is steadfast [that is, committed and focused on Jesus—in both inclination and character], because he trusts and takes refuge in You with hope and confident expectation.* (Isa. 26:3 AMP)
>
> *Then you will experience God's peace, which exceeds anything we can understand. His peace will guard your hearts and minds as you live in Christ Jesus.* (Phil. 4:7 NLT)

Thanksgiving Day arrived and the temperature again dropped below normal. The fireplace in Granny Mag's living room lit the room with warmth. Sparks skittered up the flue with glowing embers lighting from the grill to the hearth. A warmth and coziness enveloped her country home. Brett grabbed the Italian cream cake he purchased from Lamb's Bakery last evening and placed its container on the seat of the Mercedes beside him. Phyllis called him earlier that morning before she and Randy and Chrissie drove to Cooperstown.

He promised to meet them at Granny Mag's later. Brett soon left also for Cooperstown.

* * *

"I like your grandmother. Love her, really. She's both sweet and spunky," Brett told Phyllis while they stood in Granny's small but cozy kitchen with oak cabinets lining around the walls. Granny's spirit resonated in her home. A warm and loving ambience filled the kitchen and the entire house.

"I couldn't have said it better," said Phyllis. "And speaking of her, we'd better get the table set or she'll take a wet noodle to us." They both threw their heads back in a soft chuckle.

The scent of roasted turkey drifted from the oven. Granny Mag herself basted the turkey. Phyllis brought four pumpkin pies. Granny licked her fingers, tasting the tangy cranberry-and-orange relish she'd made for their dinner and gave Chrissie a spoonful who enjoyed it with one slurp.

"Let's get the potatoes whipped and finish the stuffing. Then dinner will be ready," Granny said, humming a tune and spilling her joy over the kitchen.

On the far end of the kitchen counter, Randy took the potatoes from the bag and placed them in a large bowl. Sarah Rose stood by him and peeled the potatoes.

Phyllis and Brett set the plates on the exquisite table decked with Granny Mag's tiered centerpiece made of galvanized metal trays towered in the center. Eucalyptus leaves topped with pears, pomegranates, and tangerines filled the trays. The centerpiece sat on a camel-color table runner with matching ribbons and mini pumpkins. Phyllis took in the sight of it all. Warm memories crossed her mind of the past dinners at the table. Sweet memories were made then and even more today.

"Hungry?" Phyllis asked.

Brett closed his eyes. Yes, he was starving, but for more than food. For the woman who made him feel complete, whole and loved. Yes, he was starving for a permanent relationship with her.

After the table was set and everyone took their seats. With Granny at the head of the table, she asked Brett beside Phyllis to bless the food.

Brett lowered his head and the others followed suit. He began, "Dear God, thank You for Your amazing power and work in our lives. Thank You for each hand that we hold around this table, for the food that You have graciously provided, for the nourishment of our bodies, and for Granny Mag's love and affection that she pours out to You and on us. We praise You for Your goodness and for Your blessings over us. Thank You for Your great love and care. Help us to set our eyes and our hearts on You afresh. Renew our spirits, fill us with Your peace and joy. We give you praise and thanks for You alone are worthy. In Jesus' name, amen."

Brett's prayer warmed Phyllis's heart. Each of them gave a personal prayer of thanks. Randy thanked God for bringing Sarah Rose into his life who sat beside him, thrilled to be included in the family's Thanksgiving celebration. Sarah Rose simply thanked everyone for allowing her to enjoy the holiday with them. Her sincerity could be felt. Phyllis thanked God for His presence in her life and for the love of family and dear friends. She couldn't have asked for a better Thanksgiving holiday. Granny Mag blew all of them a kiss, and they began to serve the scrumptious meal, starting with the roasted turkey. Phyllis thought that she could not have asked for a better Thanksgiving. Those with Grayson paled in comparison.

After they returned to Schenectady, Phyllis touched bases with Meredith as usual.

"Hi, Phyllis. How did your Thanksgiving go?" Meredith asked, beckoning Phyllis into the house.

Before she could answer, Phyllis took in the usual smells of cookies baking in the oven. "Cookies so soon? Christmas is a little less than a month away."

Meredith paused. "These cookies are my gift to James Werner's bakery," she said giddily. "Werner's Sweet Treats opened a couple of weeks ago." Meredith gave Phyllis a playful wink. "Now, young lady, tell me all about your Thanksgiving."

"It couldn't have gone better but—"

"But what?" Meredith asked.

Phyllis blurted, "Randy is upset. He doesn't approve of my relationship with Brett."

"What are you and Brett going to do?" Phyllis heaved a long sigh of exasperation. "Brett cares about you very much."

"And I care about him but—"

"No buts. Who do you trust when you don't have the answers? Who can and will work this out? Will you grab a hold of faith in God?"

Meredith's words hit her in the face and settled down in her spirits. "Your point is clear. I get the message. Thanks for always being a good friend," Phyllis told her. Her mood changed from questioning to upbeat in a fraction of time. She grabbed several cookies from the silver platter. "Mmm! Nothing like chocolate to fix a situation," Phyllis teased. Meredith wagged a finger at Phyllis for changing the subject but sent her a teasing grin.

Phyllis was troubled about Randy's feelings concerning her relationship with Brett. She would have to tell Brett about it. He called to tell her that he'd come by after work when she hinted that a major problem bothered her. A knock at the door silenced her thoughts. Unlike the last time, Brett stood there unsmiling. He felt that Phyllis would lower the hammer on their recent connection. A forlorn look etched his face that she ached for him.

"Come on in," Phyllis said. "I'll pour you a cup of coffee."

Brett sat at the oak leaf table in the kitchen while Phyllis made the coffee. He observed that Phyllis looked as if she had something she wanted to talk about, but he didn't know how to drag it from her. She already mentioned that something was bothering her. Neither of them spoke for a moment until Phyllis broke the silence.

"Brett, maybe we should call things off for now. Randy doesn't accept our relationship. The divorce with his father affected him. He is a troubled kid and had a recent run in with the police. It was a miracle that he didn't do jail time and only got a three-year probation with months of community work for his gang involvement."

Her comments washed over him. "You want me to do what?" His voice wasn't exactly thrilled. Although he suspected this was about to happen, he calmed himself. The frown on his face shifted to concern. He took her hands into his. "I fully understand," said Brett with a solemn nod.

Phyllis sensed that though he tried to hide it, his eyes reflected a deep hurt and inner struggle. She remembered Meredith's words and felt that Randy's problematic issue with their relationship would somehow resolve itself with God's direction. God would give her wisdom and guidance of how to handle it.

A few minutes later, Randy opened the door to the apartment. They did not hear the key in the door or him entering the apartment. Randy swung around the doorway but stepped back when he heard Phyllis mention his name. His heart rose to his throat. Brett and his mom talking about him. Neither Phyllis nor Brett still heard him although the door banged somewhat as he closed it. Randy inched close to the doorway of the living room where he could not be seen or heard. He leaned against the wall and listened to their conversation.

"Brett," Phyllis continued, "the more I think about our relationship, the more impossible it seems." Her eyes was starting to tear up. "I love my son, and I won't abandon him."

Won't abandon me? His mom's words echoed in his mind. A lump rose in his throat. Randy paid close attention to every word of the conversation. He pressed his ear hard against the wall to hear clearly.

"You know how I feel about you Brett. You've been like a gift to me. But I don't need anything or anyone to put a barricade between Randy and me. It's been hard on him."

Brett gave a single head nod. "Let me think about it, but I can see where you're coming from. Did I ever tell you my story?"

"No, I don't' recall. I'd like to hear it," Phyllis said."

"When I was in high school, I made a bad decision. I joined a gang at fifteen and was almost killed by my gang members because I wouldn't help them rob a wealthy elderly couple." Phyllis eyes widened in disbelief. "Yeah, the shy all-star football player hung out with a gang because I felt empty inside. I didn't feel accepted by the other kids, and it rocked my world. I needed to feel like I belonged and had some measure of worth. My mother and father didn't know it, of course. My folks raised me and taught me how to live life through faith in God. Out of desperation, I reached out for that faith. God turned my life around. I became a surgeon because I yearned to help others. I started Youth for Change and Progress, an outreach program, over a year ago before I came to Schenectady."

Leaning against the wall in the hallway, Randy listened furtively. Brett's story captivated him and warmed him like a blanket on a cold day. A lump formed in his throat as scalding tears streamed down his face. Hearing Brett's story, Randy began to see him differently as a person he probably could relate to in time. He felt that Brett was real. With his head lowered to the floor, he strode to his bedroom to think before they realized he had entered the apartment.

Phyllis gave Brett a comforting hug. He tilted her chin, and their lips met. As his arms drew her closer, she knew at that moment that God had ordained their reunion and would somehow fix the situation without her abandoning Randy. For once, an assurance and a comfort spread through her. His faith came so easily to him, it seemed. It dictated his actions and how he treated others. She had seen it the first day she met him and many days since. No matter how gloomy his life seemed, the promise of better things waited on the horizon.

Time passed, Brett and Phyllis's relationship strengthened. Brett wanted to reach out to Randy. He discussed the idea with Phyllis. At first, she was not sold on it but finally agreed.

On his day off from work, Brett drove to Schenectady High School a few minutes before Randy's classes would be dismissed. He understood Randy. He had been where he was emotionally. He would reach out to him and hoped it would help. He'd ask God for the words and pray Randy would accept them. Brett waited for Randy near the bus parking lot. Students had begun loading on buses. Brett stood where he could see Randy heading in his direction. From the distance, he spotted Randy's lanky form and braided hair.

"What's up? Brett asked Randy. "If you don't mind, I'd like for us to talk."

With his head lowered, Randy flipped a long braid over his shoulder. He pondered whether he'd speak. He remembered the conversation with Brett and his mom. Without further hesitation, he decided to give Brett a fist bump. "Sure," Randy said, looking up at him with a receptive response but wondered what Brett wanted to talk about.

Brett thought he saw a wan smile flicker at the corner of Randy's mouth. "Hotdogs, burgers, and fries sound okay? My car is this way," said Brett.

They strode side by side to the visitor's parking lot. During the ride, Brett navigated the conversation with more idle chatter until they arrived at Jacko's Burger and Dogs joint. The diner set the perfect atmosphere to talk. Mostly street workers and students frequented it. A cozy and pleasant ambience surrounded the place. They both ordered a beef burger, soda, and a mile high of fries. Brett told Randy about his involvement with a gang, the same story he shared with Phyllis word for word. He talked man-to-man with Randy. As Randy doused the pile of fries with ketchup, he looked Brett straight in the eyes without flinching.

"Randy, I admire your mom and, believe it or not, I respect you. Please know that I cannot nor do I have any interest in taking your father's place. I'd like for us to be friends. I'm here for you if you'd like." Brett poured his soul out and offered Randy his help. He raised a hand high in the air for a high five with Randy.

Randy slapped Brett's hand high in the air. "High five!" Randy yelled. Randy opened his once closed heart and also shared his thoughts a little at a time. "Thanks, man. I needed this," said Randy.

Today signaled the initial beginnings of camaraderie and a friendly relationship. They talked sports and chuckled about the winners and losers of the season. As always, Randy ate heartily. He could not remember when he felt this good as he enjoyed Brett and his talk. He felt less frustrated, less angry, and less confused and hurt. Even a ray hope sprang in him. He wasn't exactly sure of what hope he was looking for, but he'd know it when it happened.

Brett sent Phyllis a quick text after their meal. Both of them left Jacko's for the apartment. Brett gave Randy a manly hug, which Randy reciprocated. Inwardly, Brett gave God thanks for divine intervention and drove Randy home. He would fill Phyllis in on the details of their outing.

Like the rest of the year, the month of December flew by as well. Around mid-December, the hustle and bustle of the Christmas season became more apparent to Phyllis. Shoppers hunting for bargains in stores and others looking for the perfect Christmas tree on corner vendors signaled the season. Many of the residents in the Hamilton Hill area displayed the same festive vitality. People were hanging door decorations and shopping. In the Ridgeway Courts complex, Phyllis was curled on the sofa, making a Christmas shopping list when her cell phone rang.

"Hello, dear," said Granny Mag. "Call me spoiled, but I want you and that wonderful young man—what's his name, Brady?—and the kids to spend Christmas in Cooperstown."

"His name is Brett," Phyllis chuckled. She recalled the good times at Thanksgiving. "What should I bring? Pies, cakes, salads? I'm happy to help you as much as possible, Granny."

"No, dearie, I have *everything* covered," Granny said in a coy voice.

She dragged out the word *everything* for a long time as if she was concealing something. It left Phyllis wondering. Maybe it was something surprising about a church service. Granny Mag was not only spunky and creative, but also funny. *She's definitely up to something*, Phyllis thought.

Her mind shifted to Brett. She planned on texting him to give him a heads up about Christmas at Granny's. During an earlier conversation with him, she mentioned that Granny probably wanted them to spend Christmas with her. Brett would be elated. Phyllis mind switched again to the last Christmas she spent with Grayson in their charming riverfront home. In the spacious living room, purple accents accentuated the Christmas tree the color of a powdered donut. An exquisite skirt popped the scintillating tree with its matching faux fur. Most of their belongings had been lost in the foreclosure, including Christmas decorations. Phyllis remembered the pair of deer silhouettes for the yard that she had to leave and boxes of expensive festive decorations. She decided to purchase a small simple wreath for their apartment door. The beauty of Grayson and her home paled to the beauty of the spirit she enjoyed with Brett. She looked forward to Christmas now more than she had in years.

CHAPTER 19

HER CELL PHONE rang a second time. Granny Mag's voice greeted her. "I hope I'm not disturbing you, sweetie, but can you try to come down by Christmas Eve? There's decorating to be done, and I could use your help. Maybe Brady—I mean, Brett can also come if his work schedule allows."

"I planned on coming early since I have an entire week of vacation leave already scheduled," Phyllis said. "Brett will be out of town for several days but will return before Christmas Eve. He says thanks for the invitation and he looks forward to seeing your smiling face."

"Oh, that's wonderful! Give my love to the kids. See you soon," said Granny Mag.

* * *

In his bachelor pad, Brett turned one way then another on the sofa, looking for his buzzing cell phone. It was lodged between the pillows. He managed to grab it and answered the call.

"Son, how are you?" his mother asked.

"I'm overflowing with the joy of the Lord, Mother," Brett answered. While his response was true, he also knew that it would comfort his mother to know that he kept God's goodness in mind.

"That's always good to hear. Son, your father and I have a bit of news for you. Remember the Wilson property that we discussed sometime ago before you moved back to Schenectady?"

"Yes," Brett answered, absorbing in the conversation with a degree of anticipation.

"Well, it's yours now."

"Mother—" Brett started to protest, shaking his head.

"Now, son, not a word out of you. That young couple who rented it moved out. They are military folks, you know how they travel around. The property is too much for your dad and I. Actually, we don't need it. It's the perfect place for someone to raise a family. It's a sprawling home on the hillside with ten acres of land and close to downtown Schenectady. It's to die for! You must know it is prime property. We've put aside a nice lump sum to cover all expenses."

"Mother..." Brett could hardly get the word out of his mouth.

"No arguing with your mother. You must sign the papers before Christmas, okay?"

Silence fell over the conversation for a short while. In the words of his father, when Ruth Moreland spoke, the conversation was over. He'd have to sign the legal documents this week since next Saturday was Christmas. Brett began to relish the idea of becoming a home-owner. Could it be a sign of future blessings for him around the corner? He hoped so.

"Speaking of Christmas, your father and I are going to visit his brother who is a little under the weather. Would you like to tag along with us? Colorado is beautiful this time of year for skiing."

"Thank you, Mother, but I've been invited to spend Christmas in Cooperstown. Give my best wishes to Uncle Van. I'll come by before you leave and drop my presents off for both of you. I'll see you and Dad real soon."

Several days later, after Brett became the legal owner of 4300 Wilson Square, he boarded a flight to Washington DC for a two-day medical conference. Christmas was his favorite time of the year. Like a kid waiting for Santa to come down the chimney, his excitement escalated. He planned to visit one of the fancier jewelry stores before heading back home to Schenectady. Spending Christmas with Phyllis and the family filled him with pleasure. He and Randy talked on several occasions since their fireside chat at Jacko's. He continued to gradually open up to him. He had a long way to go to get back on track, but he was well on his way, Brett thought.

The week ended with Christmas only seven days away. Phyllis sighed as she and Chrissie headed into apartment 13F. Her Christmas vacation started this weekend. To say that she was ecstatic was an understatement. In her head, she counted the days, trying to decide the exact day they would leave for the holidays. She determined that Monday of the Christmas week was best since it gave her a full weekend to prep and pack.

Brett called earlier to inform her that he would fly back to Schenectady on Thursday, the day before Christmas Eve. He said he had to handle some business and things, but he would drive to Cooperstown on Christmas Eve. She recalled the excitement in his voice. During the entire weekend, Phyllis packed clothing and various items, including the gifts she had purchased. Monday morning after breakfast, they headed for the two-hour trip to Cooperstown, Sarah included. Phyllis tuned in to a local radio station that played Christmas carols for kids. Chrissie sang along all the way to Cooperstown. Champion slept besides her, snoring as usual.

When Phyllis pulled the Lexus into Granny's driveway, a cascade of light fluffy snowflakes began falling. Like goose down from a torn pillow, the white clumps gathered on the windshield and danced across the car's hood.

"Look, Mommy…snow!" Chrissie yelled from the back seat.

Champion was now wide awake and yapping. They got out of the car, excited over the fresh falling snow.

"Oh, it's beautiful!" Phyllis said, rubbing her bare hands together for warmth.

Sarah Rose and Randy walked ahead of Phyllis and Chrissie. Both carrying the key lime and pumpkin pies Phyllis had baked, they knocked on the door.

"Hello, everyone!" Granny Mag greeted, swinging the door wide open. She wiped her hands on the Santa Claus apron tied around her slim waist. "Come this way, I'm working in the kitchen. "Put your things down and make yourselves comfortable."

Phyllis picked Chrissie up who was licking the snow on her hands and followed Randy and Sarah Rose into the house. They stepped into the living room, and wonderful smells of Christmas filled the house—cookies baking in the oven, pine needles, and citrus scents in each room. Chrissie jumped down out of Phyllis's arms and immediately began chasing Champion around the living room. Phyllis handed Chrissie a pair of dog reindeer antlers that she bought for Champion. Chrissie placed them on Champion, which dangled sideways. The Maltese wearing the plush reindeer antlers was a sight for sore eyes. Granny Mag started untangling a string of lights on the coffee table.

On Christmas Eve, Brett arrived early in the morning laden with gift packages of various sizes and shapes. Phyllis met him at the door. Brett wrapped his arms around her waist and smothered her with a welcoming kiss. Gifts wrapped in holiday colors spilled from his arms.

"Call me Mr. Claus," he said with a broad smile as warm as the fireplace.

"Thank you for doing this," Phyllis said. She helped him set the gifts near the fireplace centered in the living room.

"How can I help?" Brett asked.

"Decorations have to be hung then we must find a tree. But first, we'll decorate."

"It's Christmas Eve, where will we find a tree?" Brett asked.

"Plenty are in the rear of Granny's property. We'll just go out back and cut one." Phyllis made a cute face and in a teasing gesture, gently slapped him on the shoulder.

Brett returned her gesture with an impish grin. "As you say, *Mrs. Claus*."

At Granny's directions, the tasks began. Randy and Sarah Rose tore into boxes of decorations lined against the living room wall. Each box contained a mix of years of new and used Christmas decors.

Brett pulled out a huge wreath that he hung adjacent to the fireplace then helped Phyllis untangle a bundle of lights. "I haven't done this in a long while."

"You haven't?" Phyllis asked in a questioning voice. "Why not? You aren't a scrooge, are you?

Brett grinned up at her. "Bachelors don't decorate for holidays." He hoped that wouldn't be the case for very long.

"What about when..." Phyllis trailed off. She realized her mistake so she stopped herself.

"You mean when Carly and I were married?" Brett finished for her. "Carly loved Christmas but chose shopping over decorating. She'd much rather flit from store to store, hoarding expensive perfumes and everything else she didn't need. Decorating was beneath her. She never learned that it's the fragrance of your life that counts, not perfume. One time, she brought us a prelit desk-sized tree in a pot. I don't know why I didn't care."

Brett's logic and wisdom warmed Phyllis's heart. She did not wish Carly any ill will but she wondered if she ever truly loved Brett. Brett tackled his last task inside the house, hanging the cluster of bells on the door so it jingled when people came into the house. Outside, he hung a giant wreath draped in silver-and-gold ribbons and wrapped garland around the winding porch. A heavy snow had fallen throughout the night. "Here you go," Phyllis handed Brett a mug of hot chocolate as she enjoyed their task of decorating together.

By midevening, Brett and Phyllis held hands while trying to find a perfect tree. The sun hung low in the sky, turning the snow to a grayish hue The last rays glinted on the ice coating the trees and power lines. An icicle dropped from a tree as they walked past, falling on the crusted snow. Phyllis's face sparkled like diamonds on a fresh blanket of snow. Even the bitter chill of winter did not detract from the Christmas spirit she felt while trudging in the snow besides Brett. Phyllis turned around to see Randy and Sarah Rose following closely behind them, laughing and playing around like kids. Chrissie and Champion stayed with Granny Mag until they returned.

Randy trudged besides Sarah Rose when suddenly, he stepped backward, reached down, grabbed a handful of snow, and balled it up. When Sarah Rose turned around, he smacked her with a snowball squarely in the face. Peals of laughter echoed in the air. Grinning mischievously, she grabbed snow off a nearby branch and threw it to Randy. Phyllis and Brett turned around at the sound of laughter. Brett eyed Phyllis and joined in the fun for a brief moment. Eventually they wiped snow from their jackets and made their way down the path where trees towered in abundance.

"Granny's property seems extensive," said Brett. As far as the eye could see were pines, firs, and maples covering the landscape. "Look! That one is perfect, a balsam fir."

"How'd you know it is a balsam fir," asked Phyllis.

"My uncle owns a tree farm in Albany, New York. We spent enough Christmases with him and his family. He taught me a few things about picking out and taking care of Christmas trees."

"Wonderful, your expertise is needed today," said Phyllis, giving him a wink.

Back at the house later, Randy and Brett hoisted the tree into its stand. Phyllis looped white lights around her hand and began draping them over the tree branches with Brett's help. Randy and Sarah Rose worked on the opposite side of Phyllis and Brett. They grabbed strings of beads and passed it back and forth as they wound their way to the bottom of the tree. Phyllis removed the tree topper out of a small box, an angel adorned in a sequined gown radiating with silvery light. Brett motioned for Phyllis to give him the topper. Holding the angel in one hand, he reached down and scooped Chrissie up who squeezed between them. He handed her the angel that she placed atop the tree, giggling with glee.

"Angel," Chrissie said.

"Just like you," Brett said and pecked her on her chubby cheek. Chrissie squirmed in his arms. He lit up like a Christmas tree. Brett always wanted children, but Carly did not. Although he was an only child, he experienced the love of a large loving family. Phyllis looked on in admiration. "The tree looks great," Brett whispered in Phyllis's ear.

"Thank you for everything, Brett," she said.

"It was fun." Brett could smell something wonderful drifting in from the kitchen. "Do you think Granny would like our help in there?"

Granny Mag emerged out of the kitchen into the living room. "We need goodies for the Christmas cantata at church tonight. I thought I'd get started. I'd love the company and help too."

"You said you were making pies," said Phyllis.

"That's right," Granny said. "We need cookies as well." She turned and went back to the kitchen. They all scurried behind her. "Aprons are in the drawer." Granny pointed to the third drawer for Phyllis to open. She gave everyone an apron. Champion sat in the doorway still clad in reindeer antlers, wagging his tail.

"Let's get started," said Granny.

The feeling of friendship and warmth exploded over Granny Mag's kitchen. Phyllis took the task of filling a tray of creamy lemon bars and sugarplum cookies that Granny already baked. Randy grabbed several and shared with Sarah Rose. Brett leaned against the kitchen counter, munching on an iced gingerbread man he'd taken from a separate platter. Several large bowls of butter, eggs, flour, and other baking items spread across the oak table. Even Chrissie joined in the fun.

"We'll have to put flour on your hands Chrissie," Phyllis said.

Chrissie reached into one of the bowls and took some dough. She giggled as her hands were coated with flour. Scratching her nose with her knuckles, she left a white splotch of flour across her nostrils. Granny rolled and floured the balls of dough. Randy and Brett cut out gingerbread men, while Phyllis and Sarah Rose cut out candy canes and an assortment of shapes for the sugar cookie dough. Granny Mag placed a small container of red and green sprinkles for the dough. The kitchen looked like a natural disaster had taken place, but they all had so much fun. They gathered in the living room when they finished the baking and had enjoyed their fill of goodies. Granny played the piano while they all bellowed Christmas carols.

CHAPTER 20

CHEER RADIATED IN the air on Christmas morning. Lively flames crackled in the glowing fireplace, sending warmth and light far out into the living room. "It's the Most Wonderful Time of the Year" and a playlist of other Christmas carols played in the background, adding to the season's merriment. Delightful smells permeated the house the whole day. An occasional roar of laughter from the dining room let Phyllis know someone was in a playful mood. Before going into the kitchen, she checked out her appearance in the full-length mirror hanging behind Granny Mag's bedroom closet. She pulled on a knit sweater with a snowflake embroidered on an ivory background to match her slacks. Her brown eyes gleamed as she styled her hair in loose curls that dangled to her shoulders. Looking into the mirror, a touch of cherry-red lipstick was added for just the right amount of makeup.

"Wow, you look stunning!" Brett said when Phyllis entered the kitchen.

"Thank you." She smiled. "*Mmm!* It smells wonderful in here," she said, sniffing. She sneaked another look at Brett, making himself at home and pouring a mug of coffee. "And you're not so bad-looking yourself," she said. Brett wore dark jeans and a forest-green pullover, with a chambray shirt underneath.

Chrissie was clad in Rudolph the Red-Nosed Reindeer pj's. She and Champion, habitual partners in crime, were harassing the golden retrievers still wearing reindeer ears. Phyllis let out a chuckle.

"Mrs. Whitmore, you look really great," said Sarah Rose. "Your outfit is stunning."

Randy sent Phyllis a flicker of a smile as his approval. He wasn't a fan of commenting on women's clothing.

"Great job," said Phyllis at Randy and Sarah Rose arranging cookies on a bright red tray on the table, which they baked the night before. They both looked dazzling. Sarah Rose wore a burgundy maxi dress, her dark hair twisted in a braid. Randy sported a black crew neck sweater that fit snugly over his broad shoulders and denim slacks.

Granny's tradition of opening presents after a late evening dinner made everyone more anxious for the scrumptious meal. Last night, Phyllis placed the gifts she bought under the tree after everyone was asleep, which included a silk tie for Brett.

"I cannot recall ever having so much fun for Christmas," Granny Mag said. She loved every minute of it. Phyllis moved around the kitchen with pep in her step, broad smiles, and more than a hug or two for anyone in her proximity. "You're glowing, dear," Granny said.

"I am for sure," Phyllis said. "It has nothing to do with the honey-baked ham or the turkey in the oven or all of this." She pointed to a pot filled with steaming hot mashed potatoes, stuffing, green beans, and six pies lined up on the counter with a three-tiered cake. Granny had more than enough food to feed an army, the navy, and all of the air force. Sweet potatoes, cranberry salad, a fresh spinach salad, turkey gravy, and yeast rolls were just a few of the dishes on the menu. There would be plenty of leftovers for her guests to take home. Granny would insist on them taking all leftovers.

After several hours of meal preparation, games, and fun, the clock struck six o'clock. Everyone gathered around the table set with the festive Christmas décor. Phyllis carried the huge salad bowl and Italian dressing to the table. Brett and Randy sliced the ham and turkey as Sarah Rose carried a platter in one hand and the bowl of yeast rolls in the other. When the table was completely set and everyone got seated, Granny asked Brett to say the blessing. Brett bowed his head and the family joined in as he blessed the food.

After the scrumptious meal, they rose and headed into the living room toward the Christmas tree. Granny gave Brett the Santa Claus outfit she had hidden away in a closet near the kitchen. Then she joined the others while Brett got dressed, giving him a wink as she left.

"Ho, ho, ho! Merry Christmas!"

Brett entered the living room from the kitchen wearing the Santa Claus suit. He threw his head back and bellowed another Merry Christmas that echoed over the room. Brett reached down, grabbed an elongated box wrapped in silver with a huge red bow, and gave it to Chrissie. She tore into the box and snatched the Baby Alive doll that giggled and sang. Santa Claus then handed Granny Mag a green gift tied with a gold ribbon.

"It's beautiful!" Granny said, stroking the multicolored silk scarf against her face. "Thank you!" She gave Santa a hug.

Brett turned and faced Randy and Sarah Rose. "Would you both open your gifts together?" he asked. They each unwrapped a small rectangular box with sparkling red paper and a green bow at the same time. They also screamed at the same time. Inside were two separate tickets for an upcoming Beyoncé concert.

"Awesome!" Randy whooped. He jumped up and down and grabbed Sarah Rose in a bear-hug. Sarah Rose teared up, wiping both eyes with the back of her hand.

Brett turned to Phyllis and gazed at her boyishly. Everyone looked on as he took his last gift from under the tree and handed it to Phyllis, an oversized octagon box wrapped in sparkling silver tied with a silver-and-gold bow. Phyllis struggled to open the oddly shaped box. A smaller one had been nestled inside of the huge box. She flipped open the smaller one. It was a gorgeous diamond ring set in 18K white gold. Phyllis let out a gasp. For several moments, she was unable to speak. "Oh!" she breathed softly, "this is wonderful!" The gem's rays glinted a brilliance of its own.

"Phyll, I love you, dear! I've loved you ever since the day I first saw you," he bent down on one knee. Will you marry me?" Phyllis heart lurched. She gave a delighted nod of consent. Brett pulled

Phyllis into his arms. Their lips met in a long sweet kiss. "I'll love you forever."

* * *

Two months later, Phyllis's heart swelled with happiness that today she and Brett would be married. They planned their dream wedding with family and a few friends on Granny Mag's farm. Brett was brimming with anticipation knowing that soon the property he recently got from his mother and father would be filled with shared love with his bride. When he showed her their future home, she could not believe that God would give her even more than she had with Grayson. Brett's joy overflowed. He now had the love of a family that he always desired and one that had become so precious to him.

Earlier that morning, Phyllis eyed the dining room table covered in a glossy silk that gave the décor a polished finish of elegance piled with trays of *hors d'oeuvres*. The wedding cake at the center of the table was a culinary masterpiece in white layers with buttercream frosting and topped with fresh red roses, lavender, and lots of decadent drizzles. It stood as a monument of love.

Later that evening, Reverend Barker stood at the head of Granny Mag's church. He patiently watched the front entrance where Phyllis would soon walk down the aisle. A broad smile blanketed Brett's handsome face dressed in a classic tuxedo. An aura of glee and love saturated the air. Brett stood next to Reverend Barker, anxiously awaiting his bride to meet him at the altar. George, Wylie, Kevin, and Oscar were perched on the front row seats to witness the joy of their only sister. Soft music played as Meredith and Charles Werner strolled down the aisle together to the altar as the maid of honor and best man. Charles gave Meredith a promising wink. She and Phyllis had discussed that they would be soon picking a dress out for her special day. Meredith returned Charles' wink.

Soon Reverend Barker asked all to stand when the wedding march began to play. Phyllis glowed as she glided down the aisle, looking glamorous in a mermaid V-necked sweep train dress adorned with beads that shimmered like diamonds on a snowy day. When they exchanged their personal vows, Reverend Barker then pronounced them man and wife. "You may salute your bride," he said, standing back.

Brett lifted Phyllis's veil and drew her closer, his arms against her back. She breathed in his woodsy citrus scent she learned to love. Their first kiss as husband and wife was sweet. Brett and Phyllis's marriage today connected the family unit again.

Phyllis could never have predicted the events of the first day of her new life. Living sane in a crazy world was more than a possibility; it was her reality.

> *And the God of all grace, who called you to his eternal glory in Christ, after you have suffered a little while, will himself restore you and make you strong, firm and steadfast.*
> —1 Peter 5:10 (NIV)

QUESTIONS FOR DISCUSSION

1. Who was your favorite character and why?

2. What life lessons, if any, did you learn from Phyllis's best friend, Meredith?

3. How did Brett and Phyllis share in their need for each other?

4. After reading this novel, do you know how to live with a greater sense of sanity through the chaos of life?

5. How would you describe Randy's real problem? Is this problem only evident in families where a divorce has occurred?

6. As a single mom, do you feel Phyllis handled Randy's situation with wisdom?

7. When did Randy's attitude really change and what part did Brett play in his transformation.

8. Mag knew her Bible and followed God's wisdom to share His word with younger women. Do you know anyone you can mentor like she did?

9. What is the single virtue that you appreciate about Phyllis?

10. What faith message did you learn from this story?

About the Author

Loujeanne Guye is the executive director of Loujeanne Guye Ministries, Inc. She is an impactful conference speaker, dynamic teacher, and life coach. She holds a masters of divinity degree from Logos University (formerly known as Logos Christian College and Graduate School) in Jacksonville, Florida, and earned a bachelor's degree in sociology from Mississippi Valley State University.

Loujeanne resides in DeSoto, Texas, but hails from Greenwood, Mississippi, the capital city of "white gold." Gemstones? No, it pertains to fields of white fluffy cotton. Greenwood, dubbed the "Cotton Capital of the World," gave Loujeanne the unprecedented story of her life. After both of her parents died when she was just seventeen, Loujeanne stepped up to the plate as head of the household raising eight siblings on 160-dollar-a-month budget while attending college and living in their apartment under her name. God's wisdom and provision is still at the center of her and her siblings' success. Always drawn to the pain of others, she aims to elevate people and empower them, especially disadvantaged youth and their families, to live a prosperous life in their quest to become productive citizens.

Loujeanne is a proud member of the Alpha Kappa Alpha Sorority, Inc. She has a daughter named Jamie and two granddaughters, Zion and Eden. Her mantra comes from 1 Kings 8:60 (KJV), "That all the people of the earth may know that the Lord is God."